WOMAN OF STONES

A NOVELLA

MEREDITH ALLARD

Woman of Stones: A Novella

Copyright © 2013; 2024 Meredith Allard

Copperfield Press

Cover design by Anna Pryce

ISBN-10: 0615832164

ISBN-13: 978-0615832166

Woman of Stones: A Novella/Meredith Allard – 1st paperback edition 2013; – 2nd paperback edition 2024

{1. Religious—Fiction. 2. Jewish Literature—Fiction. 3. Second Temple—Fiction. 4. Jewish—Fiction. 5. Middle Eastern Fiction—Fiction. 6. Jewish Historical—Fiction. 7. Historical—Fiction. 8. Literary—Fiction.} I. Title

Hatred stirs up strife,
But love covers all sins.

~Psalms 10:12

ONE

*M*y eyes were sanded shut by the wind, the sun, and the shame. I was bruised, bloodied, dragged over the rocky ground to the holy Temple where my accusers announced my impending doom. I was torn away from the man I loved because they wanted to show me my place as a sinner, to prove that I deserved to die like the sacrificial lambs led daily to their slaughter. With simple words the teacher made them leave. I felt his gaze upon me.

"Woman," he asked, "where are they? Has no one condemned you?"

My eyes opened and they leaked pain and terror as I searched the Temple court for someone, anyone, with their skull-cracking stones aimed at me. Only the stones remained, left where my accusers had stood. My hand reached for the necklace of precious jewels my husband placed around my neck but it wasn't there.

"No, sir," I said.

"Nor do I. Now go your way and sin no more."

Sin no more. As if I had ever foreseen myself a sinner, a woman soiled in the eyes of men and Moses. A woman of stones.

Sin no more. I wanted to cover him with the tears of my sorrow. But he was gone.

TWO

*I*n truth, I do not know when I first loved him. I had always known him, his kindness, his gentleness, his smile. Then finally I met him. When I knew him I began dreaming about him, dreaming there were no boundaries between us, dreaming we made each other as happy in the real world as we made each other in my dreams. One day I looked into his eyes, such sensitive eyes, friendly and deep. One day I became curious about this man I had always known yet only just met. Then he began to visit, and then I loved him. I wanted to sleep in his arms, bear his children, and live with him until we grew into many years together, our grandchildren surrounding us, keeping us warm in their love. Dreaming about him kept my mind from my loneliness, the worst kind of loneliness, the loneliness of being surrounded by people yet having no one. I was empty, and the dreams kept my emptiness at bay because I had something beautiful to dream about.

During the day I looked for him, the corners of my sight attuned to his tall, lanky frame, his movements bobbing like a fisherman's boat on the sea. I knew instinctively when he was close. My ears picked his voice out of the cacophony of street sounds, braying donkeys, and rumbling voices. During the day, my hands deep in warm dough, my mind drew pictures of him plucking at his beard with his thumb and forefinger, his mind preoccupied, his eyes somewhere else, always thinking. I had a permanent etching of his smile behind my eyes, and whenever I looked at my etching I smiled too. I was edgy and uncomfortable when he was not around, and where he was, when I was there, I felt well in the world.

All adulterers say it began innocently enough. All adulterers want to believe we don't know what happened, how it began, who made the first move, who chose to do wrong first. Look at my situation, is what I'm doing so very bad, we ask? We don't want to admit we felt more alive doing wrong than we ever felt doing right. For myself, I can only say that I was not happy and I wanted to be happy. I was not fulfilled and I wanted to be full. I may have been loved. I may have been betrayed. I want you to understand. My story is hardly new to the human heart. Think over scenes from your own life and you may see yourself in the jeering, pointing fingers of my accusers, in the sneering glares of those standing near, in the jagged, life-stealing stones held by many. You may see yourself in me. I made choices as you have choices. Where have your choices brought you? When you look over your life, are you content with where you stand now? My story is the same story others have lived, it is the same lesson others have learned. A story of stalled dreams and dreams that come true at a price. A story about dreams that are reevaluated and dreams resurrected as truth and light. I am not evil. I do not have carelessness in my heart. I am not a seducer or a Jezebel who uses men to her own devices. In my most private heart I meant to do what was expected of me, but I wanted to be loved and I thought I found that love.

I know what it's like to live for a glimpse, a smile, a nod of acknowledgment, a pass almost close enough to feel. I know how it feels to struggle to keep your face stone-set because you must keep your eyes from lighting up and your heart from shouting your truth to passers-by. I know what it's like to be near him, aware of everyone else, pretending not to see him, not to see anyone because people notice things like secretive smiles and shy, love-filled eyes. People see them and whisper them to others. Although it was dangerous I began to seek him out more often than was safe because even a few words from him were enough to fuel me until I saw him again.

Will you judge me? Will you say I was wrong to love the heartbeat smile of a beautiful man who was not my husband? Will you begrudge me the need to fill my emptiness with dreams that could have been true in another way at another time?

Will you cast the first stone?

THREE

"The Lord bless you and keep you," the priest chanted from the Temple porch. "The Lord make His face shine upon you, and be gracious to you. The Lord lift up His countenance upon you and give you peace…"

From the Court of Women I looked toward the Holy of Holies, the Temple chamber only the high priest could enter. That was where G-d was, they said. I looked around the Temple as if it were all new to me again and I was a new wife from a small village in Galilee and such glorious magnificence was the product of my imagination. I looked toward the Sanctuary and the Purification Basin. I saw the Altar and the Oil Storage. I turned away from the Place of Animal Slaughter and kept my eyes averted from the Court of Israelite Men and barely glanced toward the Place for Lepers. I stayed away from the Court of Gentiles at the edge of the Temple. I stood past the portico and up the steps of the Court of Women, watching acerbic smoke lift the burning rings of animal flesh heavenward, an odor pleasing to Him, they said. The smoke mingled with the spicy scent of incense and there was a fullness in the air like a fragrant cloud. There was expectancy among the huge limestone blocks, as if the worshippers never knew what would come next though these same traditions had been practiced for generations. Pious Jews in Jerusalem, like pious Jews throughout the Diaspora, had eyes for nothing but the Temple, a stone mountain of white marble and gold, built to glorify G-d in the finest human fashion.

The priests chanted Aaron's blessing with ardor, their words hovering above the vast Temple courts, their hands lifted above their heads, imploring His mercy and His blessings for themselves, and for everyone. The Levite Choir sang psalms over the roar of the sacrificial flames, and my lungs ached from the smoke of flesh and incense. The time of the sacrificial service was my time for prayer. I thought if I prayed quickly He wouldn't see the weakness in me I fought so hard to hide. I thought I could trick Him into looking past me, through me, not noticing I wasn't as strong as I wanted to be, not seeing I had a sinful way of escaping my loneliness. I begged Him to help me understand. Who am I? Why am I here? Is this all there is? I prayed and I listened, but I didn't hear any answers.

After services were over I crept down the steep steps, past the praying women and the gate, looking for my husband outside the Temple after the sacrificial service ended. My husband was obsessed with the sacrificial service. He went often to the Temple to witness it. Whenever I watched him I was afraid of his joy at the sacrifice, his joy at watching others suffer for his own expiation.

From the time I was a girl, in the silence of my heart so no one would know, I questioned Him about the violence. "Why must we shed innocent blood for human atonement?" I asked.

Caught, defenseless, terrified, feeling the heat from the fire against their skin, sensing that her pieces would soon be scattered into the vexed flames, the unblemished sheep or goat would bleat piteously, backing up, trying to flee, but the handler, intent on his own redemption, would drag the pathetic creature past the Sheep Gate through the central court, the Court of Israel, to the altar. The giver was intent on giving, even if it meant inflicting suffering on another life. We were taught to believe that to sacrifice meant to come closer to G-d. By giving to G-d what we valued most, we won favor in His eyes. And favor in His eyes was what we wanted most. We wanted to be closer to Him. I wanted to be closer to Him. And yet I could never understand the need for sacrifice.

"G-d is love," my father taught me. But where is He here? I wondered. Where is love here?

I closed my eyes when the slaughter began, and I pulled my shawl over my nose when the sacrificial pieces were tossed into the flames. It was such a voracious fire that priestly assistants needed armfuls of wood to keep it burning. Sometimes the animals screamed, sending bumps along my skin, recognizing their pain. Sometimes they nickered until they faded away. Sometimes they simply closed their eyes and bowed their heads, resigned to their fate. People were atoning for their sins, and they had many to atone for. As one of the priests read the Ten Commandments, many praying at the Temple could make a list of the Commandments they had broken, broken that day, even. It was an elaborate ritual, processions of music, singing of psalms, even torch dancing as the animals were marched to their deaths. On Tabernacles, the most joyous of Jewish holy days, the celebrations lasted all night. Early rabbis had said that he who had not taken part in the Tabernacles observance in the Temple had not lived.

My husband laughed when he saw me outside the Nicanor Gate, still clutching my shawl over my nose. It wasn't a pious gesture, he said, but a weak one. To reach me he had to walk around the construction sites where the outer courts of the Temple were being rebuilt after the Temple had been damaged by foreign invasion. He shouted to be heard over the haggling cries of the moneychangers and the sacrificial animal hawkers.

"Woman," my husband said, "surely even a simple country girl like yourself can learn to withstand the great scents of our Lord's Temple. Surely you cannot still be overcome by the sacrifices and the incense. They are odors pleasing to Him, after all."

He held tight to the rabbi's proverb to not speak much to a woman on the street, even one's own wife, particularly one's wife, and he wouldn't be seen talking to me in public. He looked toward the priests moving to and from the Temple, looked for one of the many holy men he had to break bread with him at our home. He flattened his shawl, straightened his fringes, centered his phylacteries, then walked to the first priest he saw near the Temple gates.

"Shalom alekh hem," my husband exclaimed, kissing the priest's hand. "Peace be with you."

"Shalom alekh hem," the priest answered. He bowed formally.

"How are you this day?" my husband asked.

"Tomorrow will be better," answered the priest. "Tomorrow I'll be slaughtering the sacrifices. It is my privilege to do so. We can never honor the Almighty enough. He deserves constant praise." The priest scrutinized my husband with pinched eyes. "The pious must always meet their duties. When we do not meet our duties we do not show our devotion to the Lord."

"I hope my dear friend does not question my devotion to the Lord."

"I do not question your devotion, only I noticed you left today without tithing. Are the markets bringing lower prices? The Lord will accept whatever you can give. You are normally the most generous of the pious."

My husband bowed as he backed away. "Oh no, my friend. You must be mistaken. The markets are well and I have tithed at every ceremony. There are days when I have given every shekel I made that day. You must have seen someone else slipping away."

The priest sniffed as if he knew the truth but wouldn't further question a successful merchant who did often make large contributions to the Temple fund. My husband was a man of indifference, but he was a man of indifference who professed to be pious, to love the Lord and to live according to His laws. During services he prayed the loudest, closed his eyes the tightest, raised his hands the highest, bobbled his torso to and fro with more kinesthetic energy, and then, like many of the pious, he left to say and do what he pleased when he thought no one would know.

While my husband spoke to some men he knew I watched the poorer worshippers leave the Temple for their homes of stone where they would continue with the necessary tasks of hard living until it was time again to worship. Wealthy men brushed past with self-importance, their tassels low to the ground, their beards immaculately trimmed, their heads dutifully covered in the presence of Him. They wore their phylacteries high next to their hearts, leather straps wound tightly around their skin, proudly, their left arms leading them through the narrow, winding streets of Jerusalem, prompting others to step aside, thinking, "That is a man of G-d there."

Most of the men who worshipped at the Temple were wealthy, but often the women who worshipped were poor. Often they were widows left behind in an arid, inhospitable land, left to fend for themselves in a world that left them no resources to fend with. In the Court of Women, where no pious man would dare cast his eyes, women were free to express all the emotions we couldn't normally share for fear of being labeled a complainer, a nag, a wet cloak, everything a good wife or daughter would never be. Silence was a virtue. Prattle, gossip, and loose talk will inevitably lead to foolishness and indiscretion, men said, and should be avoided. Since one should speak only of matters of wisdom and learning, and since women were generally not so learned as the men, many men felt women had little worthy to say. Women didn't need to utter as many prayers or read everything written in the prayer books. Women were instructed to "pray as pious Hannah prayed, silently, with heart, soul, and confidence." All Jews were subject to the command to appear before the Lord except deaf-mutes, imbeciles, children, freed slaves, the lame, the blind, and women. But women had so much sadness, anger, and frustration. So many worries. Those of us who were daughters at home had to appease our fathers. Those of us who were wives had to keep our husbands happy or else live in fear of being cast out, alone in the desert, left to linger and beg with the lame and the blind. It was considered treason against Him and a wrath against family to cuckold a husband, a crime worthy of death, but a wife could be tossed aside with the day's mess pot, left to simmer and erode until you could no longer stand the stench, until one day she disappeared and you would have never known she was there. Women who were mothers had to stay strong for their children—strong for their sons so they wouldn't think women were weak as their fathers did, and strong for their daughters so they wouldn't yet know how painful their place was in the world.

Women were restricted to domestic affairs, possessions of their husbands. The rabbis, in their wisdom, taught that women were best suited to the indoor life that never strayed from their homes. The rabbis, in their wisdom, believed women shouldn't study Torah because women don't have the self-discipline to use Torah study wisely. Women, after all, often fall into idolatrous beliefs, contrary to His very commandment against worshipping other gods. Some rabbis went as far as to say women would use their knowledge of the Torah to seduce unwary men. The wise rabbis said, "Let the words of the Law be burned rather than delivered to a woman," and "Blessed is he whose children are male, but woe to him whose children are female." Another rabbi said every man should thank G-d he hadn't been born a pagan, a proletarian, or a woman.

In the Court of Women, watching the men with their bobbing motions, like the waves of the sea, back and forth, back and forth, mesmerizing themselves, back and forth, trying to reach even one moment of transcendence, touching heaven, alone with Him, back and forth, women were able to grasp some sense of participation.

"G-d is love," I heard my father say. "In His infinite wisdom He is love."

I looked over the weeping women in the Temple, the poor and the distraught, and I didn't understand.

As the women filed past I saw him. I looked through him as though he were part of the Temple wall, an obstacle I must pass to return home. He had a young look, his face innocent, so childlike I often wondered how his beard had ever fully grown. His blameless, compassionate eyes were everywhere at once, following the sunlight shadows peering around the city stones, following the pilgrims from the Temple as they left, some proud to have honored the Lord, others pitying those who did not honor enough, the rest who gave everything they had for a moment of Divine guidance. He watched other scribes go to and from the Temple, intent on their duties. When he saw me he turned away, and I turned away, hiding under my shawl, hoping no one had noticed anything other than two people going about their tasks, he returning to the Temple, me returning to my home to bake bread and pray for understanding.

FOUR

I am from the village of Nazareth in Galilee. My earliest memories are of goldenrod sunrises scorching the sand beneath our feet, blinding our eyes and burning our uncovered skin. Nazareth was a village of farmers, the meadow grass eaten away where the sheep grazed. From the village gate we could see what we thought was the rest of the world. Our village, like most villages, wanted security in the countryside, security from scavengers, bandits, and nuisance Romans. Like other Jewish provinces, we were under Roman rule. Upper Galilee was less Roman, less urbanized while Lower Galilee was very Roman, and therefore very Greek, cosmopolitan, multicultural, and multilingual.

Nazareth was not an open urbanized center but an agricultural village, not far from the busy trade routes but far enough. We were Jews in Nazareth, and our enclosed village kept us Jews when those surrounding us in Lower Galilee were constantly falling under the influence of clean-shaven Roman pagans and flamboyant Greek philosophers. We had a view of the Rift Valley region overlooking the route of Via Maris—the Way of the Sea—along a branch of one of the busiest trade routes. Nearby Sepphoris was an important Roman center, and wealthy people lived there. The western boundary of Lower Galilee was defined by the slopes of Mount Carmel, the east by the Sea of Galilee, the north by the southern slopes of Mount Meiron at the sites of Kefar Hamaniah and Beer Sheba in the Beth ha-Kerem Valley. Though our hills were steep and difficult to pass, those eager to communicate with people on the outside managed to do so, and a lively trade route was established along the Mediterranean and the Sea of Galilee.

From the village we could see the road, who was coming, who was going, and we didn't have to walk far for our water. Grottoes lined the village with cisterns for water, presses for olives, vats for oil, and millstones and silos for grain. We had a center for the village artisans, where the carver, the weaver, the potter, the woodworker, the metallurgist, the glassmaker, the stonemason, and the carpenters had their open-air shops. Those crafts with disturbing odors, such as the tanners who worked with animal skins, were at the edge of the village. Near the end of the harvest season the farmers in the fields were seen separating wheat from chaff, ploughing, and sometimes walking two hours to reach their fields or vineyards, their wheat and barley fields, or their olive groves. Sometimes, when the harvest grew near, farmers built lean-tos in their fields, living there from Sunday mornings to Friday afternoons, arriving at their homes before Shabbat at sundown Friday. We were a poor village, some might say hand-to-mouth, destitute, but we were hardworking and faithful and we placed our trust in El-Shaddai, G-d Almighty. If you stood near the gates of the village you could hear the village elders, my father among them, debating with pointed fingers and reverential nods.

In my childhood I loved Nazareth. I loved when the morning sun blazed from mauve to yellow to pale over the evergreen oaks, the Aleppo pines, the cypress, and the terebinths, over the meadow grass and the tulips, gladioli, marjoram, and blood-red anemones that bloomed too briefly at the beginning of the hot season. The hot sky loomed over the turtle doves cooing, over the green fruit on the fig trees, over the water well where the women gathered with their stone water jugs to gossip, over the women in the courtyards or on the rooftops preparing meals, baking bread, and scolding young children, over the blacksmith, the potter, and the carpenters at work, over the unpaved road hardly wider than a camel carrying trading packs over its shoulders, over the synagogue where the rabbi stood on the front steps greeting the men who came to worship, over the red-caped, breast-plated Roman soldiers and centurions wandering lazily through, unconcerned except when taxes were due, watching with bland eyes the lives we lived in Nazareth, over the road that stretched away from us. I loved the blue-black night sky sprinkled with floating mists of light. I loved the earthy scent of the plants and the spices. I loved the southwest winds that that brought good clouds in autumn. I loved the whirlwinds that blew in off the Sea of Galilee. But I didn't love Nazareth enough.

Nazareth was not rich. It was not pretty. At the top of the hill, if you were willing to climb over the ravines and steep edges, you could look over into Sepphoris and see the glitter of the wealthy, their carriages, their slaves, their jewels, their well-groomed men, and their pampered women. As a girl, I often watched the Greco-Roman women and wondered about their lives and wished for that gold bracelet or that ruby-studded necklace that made stones look iridescent and beautiful. I learned jealousy early even though my father reminded me that Thou Shalt Not Covet was a Commandment handed down by Moses. But I wanted things that weren't mine to have. I wanted to be pampered, and in Nazareth we weren't pampered. In Nazareth, we faced extremes of subtropical weather, from hot to freezing, from fires to frosts, from rain to wind. There were frequent water shortages and burdensome taxes. There was a land tax, a poll tax, and the Romans assessed all goods going in and out of the province and demanded some for their use. Some Romans resorted to extortion and blackmail for extra income. The Jewish tax collectors who worked on behalf of Rome were branded as gentiles, sinners, human pests, and they were ostracized from Jewish society, no longer a person among people. Tomorrow was always an uncertainty, so in Nazareth we lived for the day.

My family and I lived in a house of sun-dried mud bricks sealed with undressed field stones. Our only windows were two slits high in the wall near the timber roof, kept small to let in natural light while providing security from intruders, their height keeping our house warmer in winter and cooler in summer. We slept, dined, and lived in the upper rooms while the lower rooms acted as stables for our ass, our ox, our chickens, and our fatted fowl. Our sheep and goats were kept in a pen on the outskirts of the village. The floors of our home were beaten earth. Our clay storage jars, water jugs, cooking pots, mortar and pestles, hand mill for grinding grain, and serving bowls were stored in the central room, and my mother and I had a loom to weave the wool my father sheared into blankets and cloaks. We had an open hearth to cook our meals. The upper floor, where my family lived, was reached by an exterior stone staircase and the roof of our house was enclosed by the required parapet to prevent anyone from falling. During the hot summer months my family and I would take our bedding from our rooms and sleep outside on our rooftop to enjoy the cooler air.

We lived simply, as all Nazarenes did. My father was a shepherd, my brother a shepherd's son, my mother a shepherd's wife, I a shepherd's daughter. My father never complained that he didn't have more children by my mother, though more children would have meant more hands to help him. He found calling in his work, since wasn't Jacob, who became Israel and the patriarch of the twelve Jewish tribes, a simple shepherd when he wooed Rachel and won Leah and Rachel both? My father and brother worked long hours in the midbar keeping the fat-tailed sheep under control, allowing the animals to graze and breed, shaving wool from the sheep, and carving meat from the lambs. The more perfect lambs were kept aside, special, for they would be the sacrifices made by my family to Him, the G-d of Abraham, Isaac, and Jacob, the G-d my family prayed to for sustenance. I would weep and run from the courtyard whenever my father led the sacrifices away. I often made friends with the animals despite my mother's admonitions, yet my father understood. He let me hide under the copious shade of my favorite fig tree, the one that bore sweet fruit as big as my fist, until he left and there was nothing but the memory of soft nickers and nudging fur.

He was a small man, my father, soft-spoken and gentle with the animals he tended. When the littlest lamb in the flock was left behind to die, my father took her home and made a pet of her. Tamar, he called her, like the date palm where she was found bleating her forgotten mother's name. My father knew Torah, and if we saw an animal suffering we were compelled to help it. We were forbidden to cause suffering to animals. A person was not to eat until he had fed his animals. My father quoted to us often from Exodus, "If you see the donkey of someone you hate lying under its load, you might want to refrain from helping him, but you must make every effort to help him." My father knew we were supposed to relieve any living creature of pain whether it had an owner or not. In Tehillim, the Book of Psalms, my father read, "The Lord is good to all, and His mercy is on all His creations."

"Then why the slaughter?" I pleaded.

"Even when slaughtering an animal the Torah requires us to avoid causing unnecessary pain," my father said. But I didn't understand.

My mother kept my family warm and fed. She taught me everything she knew because Jewish women were duty-bound to know the laws and regulations. She taught me the dances and the songs.

"You must know these," she said after singing a mourning song. "One time in the future you will be called upon to follow the procession at funerals, to mourn and to wail loudly for those too stunned to mourn well. Our duty is to help in mourning since only women understand the preciousness of life."

My mother showed me how to draw water. She taught me how to build fires, milk the sheep and goats, and churn the curdled milk to make cheese and yogurt. She taught me how to use the date palm for all its resources, the leaves for basket weaving, the fruit for sweets and the seeds for animal fodder, and the fig honey for fermenting into wine. She taught me how to use the olives, the almonds and the pine nuts, the coriander, the black cumin, and the cloves to make hearty meals.

She taught me how to bake bread. She showed me how to use the round grinding stones to prepare the barley. She showed me how to work the dough in a kneading trough, and how, unless it was the Feast of Unleavened Bread, to add the millet and the barley yeast, and how to leave it to rise overnight. I learned how to take the risen dough and pat it into a round, how to bake it in the mud-brick oven in the courtyard where most of the cooking was done, how to put it directly onto the embers and watch it carefully so it wasn't burned or mushy. She showed me how to make the honey donuts my father and brother ate ravenously whenever they came in from the fields and the sweetmeats of starch, honey, jasmine, and pistachio my brother and I clamored for again and again.

Bread was our sustenance. To break bread, to have a meal with someone, created a bond, made them family, and so the bread was treated with respect and there were rules that had to be obeyed. Bread wasn't cut, it was broken. Bread wasn't touched by plate, cup, or pitcher. Bread wasn't touched by raw meat. Crumbs as big as an olive weren't to be swept away but gathered. My mother found meaning in the rules. She thought the rules gave form and substance to her life, and she nourished our bodies and our hearts with her rounds of bread. In the crust we felt her protection, and in the soft, chewy center we felt her love and devotion. From a young age, when I would watch my mother bake the bread and smell the mouthwatering warmth as it drifted through the courtyard into our rooms, I saw her concentration as she gingerly touched the crust when the round came out of the oven, checking its springiness. I saw love in bread, and I looked forward to the day when I would bake bread for a family of my own. My mother taught me how to cook for the feasts and how to observe Shabbat, how to prepare the meals, how to light the candles, and how to say the prayers.

"Daughter," she said, "for Shabbat the meals are prepared with the Lord on our minds."

My mother taught my brother, too, when he was young. She taught him what he would need to know to continue our family, our name and our traditions, and she taught him every-thing from a woman's point of view, knowing full well that when he was older he would become my father's responsibility alone.

When my father and brother weren't out in the fields with the sheep, when my mother and I weren't in the courtyard washing, baking bread, or at the well fetching water, we would join together and listen to my father read Moses' Laws in his temperate voice. My father told stories from scripture like the devout man he was. My mother called him a rabbi in shep-herd's clothes.

"Even with his flocks," she said, slapping her hand into the air, "even with his flocks he is always teaching."

"There is so much to learn," my father said.

My father understood kindness. He understood forgive-ness. In synagogue he listened with his head bent forward, his shoulders slumped toward the rabbis, my brother said, as if he were trying to absorb the rabbis' way of thinking and knowing the Law. He wanted to know the Law, and he thought and he learned and he debated, first with my uncles, then, as my brother grew older, with my brother in the fields as they tended the sheep, sometimes with my mother and me.

My father told us stories from the Torah, the stories given directly to Moshe Rabbeinu, Moses our Teacher, at Mount Sinai by El-Shaddai Himself. As my brother and I grew older, we would say the stories along with him. My brother and I both loved the beginning, the Genesis, the first of everything:

In the beginning, G-d created the heavens and the earth. Now the earth was formless and empty, darkness was over the surface of the deep, and the Spirit of G-d hovered over the waters...

"From nothing there was something," my father said. "That is why we believe." I looked away from my father and he nodded.

"You do not yet believe," he said. He recited his favorite line from his favorite psalm: "Be still and know that I am G-d."

I said nothing.

"One day you will see," my father said. "One day you will learn to be still. One day you will feel Him in the stillness and understand how He loves you. Even when you do not understand His plan for you, even when you sin. Especially when you sin. G-d is love, my daughter. G-d is love."

I nodded, but I didn't understand.

From Genesis my brother especially loved the story of Joseph, how Joseph struggled until he found his calling assisting a prince of Egypt, no less. But my favorite was the story of Lilith, how she wouldn't be ruled over by Adam, wouldn't succumb to his whims, and then suddenly she disappeared, evaporated, and went to where even the rabbis did not know. In Esther's story was Vashti, who also would not obey, and she too was sent away, banished by the king, who chose the beautiful heroine Esther in her place.

"The rabbis teach these stories as lessons for untamed women," my brother said.

"What is so terrible about being sent away?" I asked.

"What if you go somewhere worse?" my mother answered.

"What if you go somewhere better?" I said.

My father laughed. "Our women do not often disappear," he said. "Our women have been destined for posterity. They have been poets, judges, prophets, great leaders of thought, great teachers of important lessons."

My mother shook her head. "Then why are we not allowed to read the Torah? Why can we not bear witness in court? The Decalogue in Exodus lists a man's wife along with his manservants, maidservants, ox, and ass as his possessions. Why is this so?"

My father never had an answer that suited her.

The stories of Adam and Eve, Noah and Abraham, Isaac and Jacob, David and Solomon, the lamentations of Job, the triumph of Queen Esther, the coming of Messiah, and how the arrival of the kingdom of G-d would end all suffering—this was how I spent my evenings with my family, my father sitting on a mat on the floor, his voice low, his arms gesticulating widely as he brought scriptures, songs, and prophecies to life, my brother watching and imitating so he could do the same for his family someday. My mother was often weaving at her loom, and as I grew older I learned to spin the wheel and helped by weaving blankets while my father weaved stories into lessons meant to guide us through the world.

"Children," my father said, "there are three basic truths we must always remember. Son, what is the first?"

"That G-d, as revealed to Moses on Mount Sinai, is the Creator and Supreme Ruler of the universe," my brother answered, smiling because he remembered the answer.

"Very good," my father said. "Wife, what is the second?"

"That Israel has been selected as the covenant people to proclaim his salvation to all the nations of the earth."

"Yes," my father said. "Daughter, what is the third?"

"The Torah is the inspired word of G-d and it sets down the principles of human morality. Torah shows us the special rules and laws Jews should live by."

My father nodded. "Very good, Daughter."

I wanted to understand the lessons in the stories. I saw the brilliance of them, the divine guidance tucked into the riddles, hidden jewels glistening within jagged sand rocks, but still I felt empty inside. My hands were busy baking bread, washing, cooking, weaving, getting water, my time full with tasks. My body was weary and my heart felt empty. My eyes constantly wandered from here to there, searching for some unnamable something that would make me understand this G-d of love my father insisted upon. To all who looked, I was a dutiful daughter, but inside I grasped for some inchoate something. I worked alongside my mother until I was too tired to think of anything but rest.

During prayers, when my eyes should have been closed, I watched my father and brother, their waving motion making them peaceful like the sea, the rhythm revealing their devotion. I watched my mother, her hands covering her eyes so that nothing earthly could distract her, and I saw her connectedness and I knew I was supposed to feel the same. But there were so many things to remember.

My father learned much from his rabbi. The synagogue in Nazareth wasn't as spectacular as the Temple in Jerusalem, but in Nazareth the rabbi taught heart-truths, personal lessons with heart and mind and G-d together. Every week my father and brother visited the synagogue to hear the Torah read. They offered up their humble prayers to the Father in heaven, the giver of Life, and my father himself would sometimes speak. My brother would have fun telling us how our father often talked to the sheep in the fields about the principles he learned in synagogue.

"G-d has created the universe and all life," my brother said, mimicking my father talking to the chewing sheep. "He has created a wonderful world for us to enjoy. G-d is goodness. We can be good too." My brother extended his hand, imitating our father patting a sheep's head. "Whether we use that goodness or not is a choice we make each day."

My father was neither Pharisee, who believed in meticulous observance of the Law combined with extreme inner piety, nor Sadducee, the wealthier Jews who lived mostly in Jerusalem, supported the priesthood, and believed in the literal truth of Torah though they had no belief in the existence of angels or the coming kingdom of G-d. My father wasn't Essene, a semimonastic group that aimed to live free of worldly corruption, that believed in ritual purity through frequent bathing, and were vegetarian because they wouldn't kill.

"I follow G-d," my father said, "and G-d is neither Pharisee nor Sadducee nor Essene. G-d is All and One."

When pressed into taking sides, my father said, "I am a free-thinking Pharisee, as our rabbi is. Our rabbi offers comfort in a suffering age. He helps us to understand our chance for repentance. He helps us to understand the love of a merciful G-d who is ready to receive the sinners. Our rabbi looks forward to the coming of Messiah. What can be better than the coming of Messiah?"

The rabbi taught that the law was given to lighten man's burden, not add to it and that our duty consists in loving G-d and loving our neighbor even when it is not convenient to do so.

"G-d is love," my father said.

Every week on Shabbat my brother would ask my father's favorite question, and my father delighted in answering him.

"Abba, what is G-d's goodness?"

"The wisest of rabbis say that G-d's goodness is lovingkindness. You should love your neighbor as yourself. Do not do to others what you do not want done to yourself. El-Shaddai teaches us to be thoughtful of the stranger, the eyes for the blind, the feet for the lame, and the caretakers of the poor." Always, looking at me, his eyes full with a father's compassion, he said, "And lovingkindness is extended to all His creations, as well."

My father passed on to us his rabbi's teachings about stones that had been sharp and had been cut but had been worn down by the elements until they reflected light. When, after spending an afternoon peering into Sepphoris, I complained that we were so very poor and uninteresting in Nazareth and hardly worthy of stories, my father said, "What does it matter that your personal lot should be commonplace? You have a privilege no power on earth can take from you. You are an ally of G-d. G-d used to speak to us through burning bushes. Now He speaks to us through our lives. What is He saying to you?"

"G-d speaks to us through our lives?" my mother asked. She rubbed her careworn hands together, hands that were sunscorched and lined like the ridges of the desert. "My life is like stones, weighted down and hard. Everywhere I see there are taxes and debt, subsistence and illness. We, the peasants, work endlessly, supporting Rome's privileged. Three of my five babies have died. I love you, Husband, and I love your devotion to the Almighty, but tell me honestly. I must know. What can the kingdom of G-d do for me when these stones bring me nothing but heartache and tears?"

"The Psalm says that G-d has tears in a bottle," my father said, "and tears are what He uses to create stones. Tears are used to reflect the sun and create rainbows. To be denied tears is to be denied the gifts He has for you. Our prophets teach us that the coming kingdom will be the end of all sorrow and all suffering. All will be perfect in the sight of G-d. The stones are merely a means to an end."

A faint smile played on my mother's lips. How she loved her rabbi in shepherd's clothes.

"One day Messiah will come," my father said. "One day Israel will again be an independent nation as it was during King David's day. There will be universal peace and justice. There will be no hatred, no strife, no suffering from human sins. Only love. One day."

My father smiled deeply inside himself, comforted in his knowledge. Then he looked at me and sighed.

"You still do not believe," he said. "G-d will speak to you strongly, Daughter. Since you do not hear his whispers now,

He will need to be more direct with you, perhaps even scream in your ear or drop a stone on your head. But you will believe. One day."

"What is it I will believe?" I asked.

"That G-d is love," my father said.

FIVE

*M*y husband often had the rabbis and the priests, the scribes and the merchants to our home to break bread. Hardly a night passed without guests to share the evening meal. Whenever someone new arrived at our home my husband took great pride in showing his guest around. Jeremiah the Scribe was no exception. He was a widower from Caesarea, Jeremiah, recently moved to Jerusalem, and he had come with the highest praise from his elders. Jeremiah was younger but much respected for his intelligence and his ability to make difficult religious concepts easy to follow, and my husband took great pains to court the scribe and bring him into his social circle. My husband cultivated relationships with men he believed would be beneficial to himself.

I trailed behind while Jeremiah the Scribe followed my husband and two acquaintances, one a rabbi and one a priest, as they elbowed their way through the crowded streets toward our home. My husband enjoyed pointing out landmarks and points of interest to his new friend the scribe. After all, Jerusalem has been the Jewish Holy Land since King David conquered the city and made it the capital of the Israelites. Like layers of time, the city had been created haphazardly, houses of the poor here, the wealthy there, markets near the city centers, a vague gloom in the shadows of the crooked, narrow streets, the Goliath structure of the Temple looming above it all. Below the bridge stretched a great paved square surrounded by colonnades. To the north was the old palace of the Asmoneans. We walked the broad causeway of the central hollow of the Tyropoeon, then crossed the bridge that connected the Temple to the Upper City where we lived.

Whenever I needed air to breathe I left through the city gates to the hillside garden on the Mount of Olives where there were flowers, green, azure skies, and curling olive trees to think under. In the city itself there were few open spaces. Every inch of land was used for homes and shops, and the crowds pushed their way past others, muttering the whole way. Soon we saw where the poorer homes—carved out of the stones of the city steps or covered with reeds and beaten earth—morphed into tiled houses in the Upper City where the aristocrats lived. When we passed the high priest's house my husband smiled at his guests.

"I am still seeking to have the high priest break bread with me."

The high priest was the supreme of Jerusalem aristocracy. His residence boasted a large courtyard with a doorkeeper, servants, and granaries for the wheat tithes, and my husband's eyes grew wide with envy. Our home, though not far away, was modest by such standards. My husband was hardly an aristocrat, his father's family having been shepherds back, he insisted, to the time of Abraham. His people had been, he insisted, among the first to follow after G-d had chosen Abraham as the leader of His nation, the first to accept the covenant.

At home my husband led his guests to the roof, from where we had a splendid view of King Herod Antipas' voluptuous palace and the Temple itself. I too loved the sight. In the evening hours when the sun began to languish in the fading red-gold sky, when my bread was baked, my home clean, and my husband tended to, I would climb onto the roof and watch the glowing prism reflect luminescent off the golden Temple and the mountains and hills beyond.

My husband glowed when he showed others the splendor in which we lived. When he felt our luxurious surroundings were not enough to enthrall his guests he boasted of me. He enjoyed telling his guests about his stubborn wife who insisted on baking his bread herself.

"She's from Nazareth," he explained, "a country girl with country ways, and she won't allow me to obtain a second servant to take care of the household needs. She must bake the bread I eat, and doesn't she bake the sweetest, springiest bread? She doesn't want me eating bread that comes from any other woman's hand. She is the jealous type, you know. She is attractive with her rustic accent, is she not? Look at that ruby necklace she wears. I gave it to her so she would not forget where her loyalties lie. She hasn't once removed it from her person."

He would wink at the men, and they would clasp him on the shoulder and say how lucky he was to have such a righteous wife.

That evening, my husband gathered with the rabbi, the priest, and Jeremiah the Scribe over wine, grapes, and cheese as they waited for their meal. Jeremiah was in the place of honor to my husband's right, and he joined the others as they dipped their bread in seasoned olive oil and talked around mouthfuls. My husband and his guests spoke of two men, new to Jerusalem, who had begun worshipping at the Temple, one an importer of Asian spices, the other a day laborer from

Caesarea. My husband, the rabbi, and the priest were not impressed.

"He wears his tzitzit too long," said the rabbi.

"His prayer shawl looks too new. He's hardly worn it," said the priest.

"They'll never make it in Jerusalem society," my husband said, dismissing the new men before even meeting them.

For my husband, the preoccupation with social standing and position was about his livelihood. My husband's richly woven textiles adorned the figures of some of the wealthiest Jewish and Greco-Roman women. If he didn't cultivate highly influential companions he wouldn't have his textiles placed in the most exclusive tailor's hands. And if he couldn't sell his textiles for a high profit, then he wouldn't make the money he needed to be in high society, and then in his mind he would be no one. In order to maintain his place, my husband, and others like him, had to make sure others didn't rise to misplace him. The way they prevented others from rising was to put them down in company, call out their faults, and create imaginary faults while spreading rumors. It was their way of making others look small so they would look large.

"What do you think of the newcomers to the Temple, Jeremiah?" my husband asked.

Jeremiah shrugged, a neutral gesture. He leaned on his left arm, the sofa close to the low table, dipped and chewed his bread, sipped and swallowed his wine, and listened. Normally, when the men argued, trying to out-shout and out-gesture each other, proclaiming their keen observations, Jeremiah the Scribe nodded his head here and waved his hands there. Jeremiah anticipated what those around him would say. He finished your sentences and gestured widely with his hands to emphasize your words. He understood you intuitively. He became a scribe because of his family tradition and his fine education, but he earned respect because of his talent, intelligence, and generosity. He was levelheaded and not easily excitable. When he spoke he leaned toward whomever he was addressing. Mothers found him suitable husband material for their daughters, but Jeremiah was a widower and he used his mourning period to shield himself from prying matchmakers.

I didn't need to serve the men, we were wealthy enough to have servants for that, but I enjoyed listening to their conversations and so I helped carry the dishes. In company I was invisible, the arms and legs that brought food and poured wine. Sometimes I glanced at my husband to see if he was pleased, but all I saw were wine glasses and empty serving dishes. But I listened. I listened to their discussions about the law. I listened to their praises of things going well and their disdain with people who had yet to do their bidding. I heard them say their prayers before and after meals, and I heard them gossip like women around the water well. Their jeers were typically directed toward other men who were not as pious as they were. Religion was the same as social standing as far as my husband and his acquaintances were concerned. They were compelled to show themselves holier, wiser, better learned than others. That night they were angered by the Roman governor, Pontius Pilate, a tyrant who was not opposed to going over his superiors' heads in Rome.

"We must be on our best behavior," said the priest. "We cannot give the Romans cause for concern."

"Simply by our existence we give Rome cause for concern," my husband said. "We follow El-Shaddai, G-d Almighty. They have their pagan gods who conduct themselves no better than the average idiot. By following our faith we are gnats in their eyes."

"Yes, but the Romans are different," the priest said. "We must be especially vigilant. They will not allow us to disrupt their Pax Romana, their Roman Peace." The priest held his wine cup high with his short arm and nodded in my direction. "As if a people who govern by the sword can ever find peace! This governor, this Pilate, he seeks any excuse to place us under his ruling hand. He has not been shy about hiding his hatred of the Jews. He thinks we're uncivilized and he'd like nothing more than to force us to worship his ludicrous pagan gods."

"It will never be done," the rabbi said. "Caiaphas knows how to handle them. He knows what to say to the Romans so they'll leave us alone as they have in the past."

"Of course Caiaphas knows what to say to the Romans," said Jeremiah the Scribe. "The Romans appointed him."

"The Romans will never leave us alone," said the priest. "Not only is Pilate a raving lunatic, but he has the full weight of Imperial Roman authority behind him. Here, Pilate is Rome, and that is bad news for us. If he wants to raid our Temple treasury to repair an aqueduct, he does. If he wants to send his soldiers out to trample Jews to death, he can. I was here when he sent out his troops with those heretical standards showing their emperor as G-d. He was doing it for no reason other than to taunt us, and when we objected he threatened a massacre!"

"But he was stopped," my husband said.

"He wasn't stopped until we fell before him with our necks laid bare," said the priest. "He realized we would gladly die rather than have our holy city overtaken by the Romans, and he didn't want to have to explain such a massacre to his superiors in Rome."

"I'm surprised even that stopped him," said Jeremiah the Scribe. "Pilate has a reputation for torturing men to death without trial."

"Can we not look to our own king for support?" the rabbi asked. "Where is Antipas during these raids?"

"King Herod Antipas!" My husband's whole body shook with laughter. "Fine King of the Jews he is! He's just another Roman puppet. He will never support the Jewish people."

"And there has been talk," said the rabbi. He emptied his wine in one swallow but shook his hand when I tried to refill his cup. "The Romans are worried about that rabbi, the one from Nazareth who gathers crowds, the one they say does miracles."

"And he is coming here," my husband said. "He is coming to Jerusalem."

"Are the Romans worried?" asked Jeremiah the Scribe.

"The Romans have reason to be worried," the rabbi said. "Have you heard his latest miracle?" Cynicism cracked the rabbi's voice. "They say he has raised a widow's son from the dead. In Nain! And people believe it! There are Jews who believe a man from Nazareth can raise from the dead! As if Messiah has come! But we know only El-Shaddai can raise from the dead."

The rabbi grew red-faced. He lifted himself with some difficulty from the low-lying sofa and paced the room. "They dare to call him the Son of Man! They say he fulfills the prophecies because he speaks with authority! Blasphemer!"

"He is one of a hundred so-called messiahs," the priest said. "He's no different than the others. Why is everyone so bothered by this one? Why are his miracle stories any more worrisome than anyone else's?"

"He is different because people listen to him," my husband said. "Just as the Baptist before him was dangerous. People listened to him too. The crowds are full of people who are willing to follow him. You are only dangerous if people are willing to follow where you lead."

"You are more dangerous if you lead in the wrong direction," the rabbi said.

"I have heard he helps those in need," said Jeremiah the Scribe. "Making a scapegoat of this one itinerant teacher doesn't help us in our quest to live as El-Shaddai would have us. Rabbi Hillel the Elder said, 'Whatever is hateful to thee, do not do unto others.'"

"But this itinerant teacher doesn't follow the regulations of the Sabbath. He eats with the unclean, with the sinners and the diseased, with tax collectors! What respectable man eats with tax collectors?"

"He has many followers," the priest said. "Many are afraid he'll lead them in rebellion against Rome. And Rome won't be happy."

I ladled more wine into the pitcher. As I turned toward the men, I heard the priest say to my husband, "Your wife is from Nazareth. Does she know this latest miracle worker?"

"No," my husband said. "She says she doesn't know him."

"He's simply another delusive vagrant looking to stir up the masses. We should be spending our time in prayer and living according to Jewish laws, not inciting the masses, putting ideas into their heads and making them impatient for change. We must accept what is. After all, we know nothing. G-d Almighty is never shortsighted. We are where He put us, we are here for His reasons, and we shouldn't question. 'The Lord is my shepherd, I shall not want…'"

Jeremiah the Scribe shook his head, an indiscriminate movement he meant no one to see. But the rabbi, his sharp eyes catching everything around him at once, flared his nostrils in the scribe's direction.

"Yes?" the rabbi asked. "Do you disagree with King David's psalm, or do you not think El-Shaddai knows of which He does?"

"I have complete confidence in El-Shaddai," said Jeremiah the Scribe. "I struggle every day to live my life according to His teachings. G-d Himself is the only true authority. It's humanity I struggle with, human judgment and human arrogance. Isn't it possible, after all, that this rabbi who is looked upon with such scorn is doing more good than harm? Who is he harming? All I hear is he heals the sick and brings hope to the hopeless."

"Making the blind see!" the rabbi exclaimed as he lay back on the sofa. He dipped his bread into his sarcasm and took a bite, his lips pulled into a smirk so sinister I thought El-Shaddai should see the rabbi then, Satan-like in his resolve. "No one but El-Shaddai has the power to make the blind see."

The rabbi quivered as he held up his cup. I steadied my hand so I could refill his wine without dripping liquid onto him.

My husband tried to lighten the mood. "We could use that rabbi here now. We're about to run out of wine." His was the only laughter and it was hollow and landed with a dull thud.

The rabbi stared at Jeremiah the Scribe. "You young men think every so-called miracle worker has the answers. The answers have been given! To Moses on the mountaintop! You are like those heretics who pushed Aaron to build the golden calf. They danced before it, singing and shouting 'These be thy gods, O Israel!' Moses turned from them for a moment and they had already forgotten the Lord's commandments."

The rabbi raised himself. He towered over the others as they reclined on the sofas. My husband stood, too, trying to help the rabbi calm himself.

"My friend," my husband said, "our young scribe meant no harm."

"No harm? He wants to dismiss all we hold holy!"

"Jeremiah, tell him." My husband pleaded with his eyes.

"I mean no harm," Jeremiah said, holding his hands out, palms up in a gesture of peace. "I only mean that different people see the same things differently, and both can be right."

37

"I should have you dismissed from the Temple! Blasphemer! Why don't you become one of his bandit followers! As if you understand the law well enough to explain it to a goat!"

Jeremiah the Scribe smiled. I wondered if it was the first time I had seen a man smile. The men I knew were guarded, closed, as if protecting the little-known secret that they were human after all. Where women smile to hide uncomfortable feelings, men smile when they are sincere. Or so I thought at the time.

The priest nodded in my direction, and I refilled his cup, spilling red droplets, like splatters of blood on rocky ground. My husband didn't seem to notice, or if he did he ignored it. I wiped the spill with a rag and backed away.

Our serving girl brought out the evening meal, roasted lamb with hot mint sauce and a salad of lettuce, mint, coriander, and chives. She served the men their meal and I poured their wine while they continued to discuss religion and politics, which were synonymous then. Jeremiah the Scribe had a point to make and he wouldn't be deterred.

"We are quick to anger G-d Almighty with our human arrogance. We say all is in G-d's hands, that we know nothing, yet too often we project our human shortcomings onto Him and we see Him as vengeful when we ourselves are vengeful. We see Him as selfish when we ourselves are selfish. The Almighty makes it clear what is best for us, and still we don't follow His path. We justify ourselves. We say we know better when we don't. We cannot trust ourselves, fallible, foolish creatures we are, to do the right thing on our own. Too often, despite our best intentions, we will be led astray because our human desires outweigh our best intentions. And still G-d forgives us. He forgives us faster than we forgive ourselves." Jeremiah paused, flickers of confusion behind his eyes. "Many of us carry guilt when it is no longer necessary. I know G-d forgives me. I know G-d understands more about my selfish desires than I do."

"We are all sinners," the rabbi said. "Jeremiah bar-Ezekiel, you are familiar with the fall?"

"Yes," Jeremiah said. "We have all fallen."

"Not everyone," said the rabbi. "But for those who have fallen it is always because of woman."

"Women bewitch us," my husband said. "Our prophets say so. Isaiah called women vain, voluptuous, and forward. Amos called them cruel, and Ezekiel said they were two-faced. Rabbis call women greedy, idle, jealous, quarrelsome, eavesdropping behind doors, gossipers that they are. Friends, a woman caused the fall of man. Eve could not resist temptation, and then she tempted Adam in her turn."

Jeremiah the Scribe stroked his beard as he considered. "But what about the proverb that says a good wife is a treasure found?"

"Spoken like a widower," my husband said. "But Jezebel persuaded her husband to do wrong, just as Eve did." My husband's fingers twisted the bread in his hands, stopping only after the rabbi grimaced at him. "Such women should be stoned, a lesson for everyone always." He glanced in my direction. "When I first brought my wife here, I showed her Golgotha. 'This is where the women are stoned,' I told her. 'This is where the unscrupulous are killed.'"

"And what was her reaction?" the rabbi asked.

"She's such an innocent country girl," my husband said. "She asked me, 'Why does G-d allow such violence?'"

"And you responded…?"

"Because we are sinful."

Again I spilled the wine. My husband saw. Everyone saw. As if my blood flooded the table for all the world to see.

SIX

I was eighteen, three years past marriageable age when he arrived in Nazareth. He traveled with a caravan of other textile traders, looking for shepherds willing to share wool for profit. The first time I saw him I was at the market as he approached from the outskirts of the village. I smelled the sourness wafting from the tanner's open-air stall, and instantly I associated the burning-flesh odor with the man with the acridic grin. He had seen me, too, and inquired about the girl who scurried away.

He arrived at our home the next morning dressed in a cloak of embroidered linen with a basket of exotic fruits and expensive spices. My mother met him in the courtyard with an iron-studded thresher in her hand. He politely requested my father's presence. My mother lit the clay oil lamp so we could see the man better, and while our eyes adjusted my mother gathered nibbles to eat for our important guest, important because he came bearing gifts and talking money. My mother brought a water-filled basin to wash his feet and she poured scented oil on his head. He thanked my mother and glanced at me as my brother rushed out in search of my father, eager to tell him of our unknown guest. Something captivated me about our visitor. He wasn't handsome, though intensity flashed behind his ash-colored eyes, a strength that dared everyone to be as forthright and determined as he. I was curious about him, and he was curious about me. Wherever I looked there he was, turned in my direction, watching me, prying into my most simple movements, seeing how I looked when I stood over the stone hand mill grinding grain, seeing how I reacted when my brother rushed into our rooms tracking sand and mud after the floors had been cleaned. What was I like when the bread burned? I enjoyed the attention even if I felt constrained under his gaze. My vanity blossomed. I imagined myself a beauty with black curling hair like Beloved in "Song of Songs." I wanted to marry this man.

When my father arrived from the midbar, staff in hand, panting from his run over the rocky, grassy knolls, he saw the stranger and stopped.

"I am Othniel bar-Ismael," the stranger said. "I am here on business. I hear you are a respected shepherd here."

"That is what is said," my father answered.

"Yes." Othniel bar-Ismael glanced in my direction. "I believe we can help each other."

It was three hours before my father and the man came out of the room where they closed themselves away. They left immediately for the synagogue, as my father would not embark on any new venture without the rabbi's consent. They prayed together, my father said, and then they broke bread together, and that sealed the deal. My father would provide cotton for the textile dealer at a fair rate, and my father would receive a monthly income from the profits for his trouble. The textile dealer wanted something else in trade, as well, but he hadn't mentioned that yet to my father. That would come later.

We saw Othniel bar-Ismael frequently as he lingered around our home. My brother looked up to Othniel bar-Ismael with obvious adoration. This Othniel, he had traveled to Crete, Athens, Syria, and even Egypt. He was traveled and learned. He lived in Jerusalem, which my brother had seen when he and my father traveled to the Holy City for the Passover celebration.

"And he lives there!" my brother said as he related the sights, sounds, and smells of the stone-made city in the nook of the hills to me. To my brother, because Othniel bar-Ismael lived in Jerusalem, that made him one of the cultural elite. Ever since my brother traveled to Jerusalem he dreamed of living there, and since meeting our guest he decided he would leave shepherding behind and become a prosperous merchant too. My father did not discourage the idea. Whatever misgivings he had about my brother's plans he kept them between himself and G-d.

Jerusalem had everything we didn't, my brother insisted— luxuries we couldn't even imagine: the gilded Temple, the Antonia Fortress, Herod's Palace, the affluent homes in the Upper City. Othniel bar-Ismael often related details of the fine meals he had shared with very important people, priests, rabbis, and the men of the Sanhedrin themselves, the council of 71 pious men who formed the highest authority for the Jewish people.

"Always, we obey the kosher laws as you do in Nazareth," our guest said. "We are pious Jews in Jerusalem, after all. We sacrifice to Him at the Temple itself."

I loitered near the men while they lounged and ate, listening to the visitor relate tales of his adventures in foreign lands. He spoke Greek, was on a friendly basis with the most important men of the day, and he knew a good business deal when he saw one. In the silence of darkness, when the day's work was done, the bread baked, my family fed, I'd slip onto the roof of our home and watch the passers-by, the men on their way home from cultivating the fields, working in their shops, tending the sheep, the women rushing home from the market, determined to be in their homes before sundown when the evening meal was expected. After our guest arrived I saw everything differently, with a detached interest, wondering if the villagers' task-filled lives had to be my destiny. Were there other options for me?

I began to daydream, filling the empty space behind my eyes with visions of myself as a grand lady. I watched the wealthy women tended by polite servants. I wanted to be one of those ladies and not have to work with my hands. Their hands looked soft and delicate, unused and proper. My hands were rough, calloused from banging ceaselessly on stones. I envisioned myself living in Jerusalem without a single chore to tend to, wearing cassia perfume, its brisk scent dabbed behind my ears, the oil scented with lily, jasmine, and rose. I was scolded by my mother whenever I listened to Othniel bar-Ismael when I should have been weaving, baking, cleaning, or preparing meals. But I was impressed with this man's ability to know what he wanted and the determination that allowed him to go after it. What he wanted, I soon learned, was me.

He regaled me with details about the wealthy Jewish women in Jerusalem, about what luxury they lived in, about their ornate embroidered, dyed robes not of cotton but of linen, and they had not only one robe but two or even, for the most wealthy, three. He told me about the jewels, the solid gold bangles the women wore on their wrists and ankles, the rubies and lapis lazuli that glinted from their necks and ears. The women wore "Jerusalems of Gold"—a necklace with a heavy crown pendant showing the holy walls of the holy city. The wealthy women had alabaster flasks of costly oil of spikenard.

They wore face powder, their temple veins outlined in blue, their lashes painted brown or black, and their eyelids painted with kohl.

"The association of cosmetics with women of ill repute isn't as prevalent among upper-class women," Othniel bar-Ismael told me. "The upper classes can do as they wish because who will tell them otherwise? These women are quite pampered. They can check their looks with glass mirrors of polished silver or gold. Maids paint their fingernails and toenails white. They have hairdos so intricate it's unlawful to undo them on the Sabbath because it would be like demolishing a built structure. Their homes have private mikvahs and the rooms are decorated with intricate mosaic floors and alabaster tables. Such ladies have servants and their servants have servants to care for everything—the home, the cooking, the children."

"Even to bake their bread?" I asked.

Othniel bar-Ismael laughed. "Yes," he said, "even to bake their bread."

"So what do these women do all day?" I asked.

"They oversee their household servants, make certain that their household follows the regulations placed before us by the Almighty, take care of their husbands, and make good hostesses when guests arrive."

Othniel bar-Ismael then tempted me with the meals he ate daily in Jerusalem. "No rough grain bread there," he said. "Only bread of the most delicate flour."

In Nazareth, we had a lunch of bread, olives, and figs. Our dinner after sunset, when the whole family came together, was a one-pot stew of vegetables served in a common bowl, sopped up with bread. Other nights we ate a thick grain porridge or a stew of lentils seasoned with herbs. In Jerusalem, I learned, the upper classes drank the best wine imported from Cyprus and ate hens' eggs and lamb roasted over the wood from the vine.

In Nazareth, we ate a diet of bread and salted fish or fish preserved in halmé.

"In Jerusalem," he said, "every night is a feast among the wealthy. Often the wealthy try to out-do each other in offering the finest local or imported foods that money can buy: exotic fruits such as oranges or lemons, roast lamb, pear compote with dried pears boiled in wine and water with honey, dried apples mixed with toasted sesame seeds, pomegranates."

He turned his ashen eyes onto me and his face hardened. "The woman I marry will find no limits to the luxuries I'll offer her," he said. "She will have the finest clothes, the finest foods, the finest company. I have influential friends. I'm personally acquainted with each of the 71 members of the Sanhedrin. I can hold my head high as a person among people, and my wife would be envied among women."

Suddenly, my loneliness, the emptiness clinching my heart disappeared in girlish daydreams. If I were the wife of an influential man in the influential city of Jerusalem then I would no longer be unnecessary or secondary, an unmarried daughter of a simple shepherd. I might be seen, and if I were seen then I would be important in the world. I saw no importance to my life in Nazareth though I saw importance everywhere in Sepphoris. In Jerusalem, I would have a position in society, unlike in Nazareth where I spent my days wiping dust from my brow with browned, calloused palms or working until my back ached. I would no longer have to sweat and labor. I imagined myself in Jerusalem, walking like a princess from my own exotic home to the exotic home of another wealthy mistress to the home of the high priest himself. What a noble man this Othniel bar-Ismael must be, I thought, that he keeps company with such people.

He always arrived at our home with expensive gifts. For my father and brother he brought the finest prayer shawls. For my mother he brought imported fruits like oranges and lemons and a perfume of oil, bark, and flowers blended to sweet perfection. He quoted Proverbs as he handed the gift to my mother: "...scented oil and incense make the heart glad..." My mother beamed with delight, and she laughed as she dabbed a pinky-nail amount of oil behind her ears. The scent of daylight flowers and warm sun sprang through the room. My father laughed, too, with appreciation for this visitor who knew the council members of the Sanhedrin, and had brought such joy to this small family from a humble village. But my father saw something more I wouldn't or couldn't see. My father saw the truth in hard-learned lessons.

At our betrothal my intended brought a special present for me, which he handed to me with great pride. My parents must have known what it would be because they watched my face when Othniel bar-Ismael thrust the necklace of blood-red rubies toward me.

"Allow me to clasp it around your neck so I may see how the jewels radiate against your beauty."

As I raised my hair I saw how the jewels sparkled in the dwindling daylight. I smiled because it looked like the glittering necklaces I had seen around the necks of the wealthy women I had envied. Now I would be envied. Othniel bar-Ismael fastened the chain around my neck.

"Hold on tight to this," he said. "Now, with your father's consent, I will marry you. These stones bind you to me and you will be known as mine forever."

I looked at the shimmering prisms in the straggling rays of light and sighed aloud at their beauty. Nazareth, my home, the only home I had ever known, was suddenly common and dull. It wasn't precious the way these color-filled stones were precious. Othniel bar-Ismael would take me away from the dust and the aches and the pains.

When it was time, my betrothed signed the contract declaring our union with my father and his brother as his witnesses. My father received a bride price, shekels of silver, though he said no amount of money could replace me in his home. "I will miss you dearly," my father said. It was the only time I cried at the thought of leaving.

My father and my betrothed signed the contract in the middle of the month since it was believed that a full moon brought good luck. When my betrothed signed the document he stated that as his wealth increased then so would his standard of living for me. Then my betrothed gave me the gifts I would use if I became a widow. The necklace of stones was among those gifts. The rabbis say all marriages should begin in the right way. Marriage isn't simply a civil contract, they say, but a sacred duty and a great privilege. It isn't good for the man to be alone, they say, quoting Genesis, "I must make a helpmate for him..." G-d created Eve from Adam's rib and then gave her as a gift to him, decreeing that man and wife must become one flesh. The betrothal is a promise of marriage, a document as binding as the marriage itself, and at the betrothal I became the possession of Othniel bar-Ismael, forbidden to all others on pain of death. Then Othniel bar-Ismael returned to Jerusalem to prepare our future home, and I collected the homemaking items I would bring with me.

One afternoon my mother and I had the talk that all caring mothers give their daughters. My mother taught me that as a wife there were duties I was obligated to perform: grinding flour, washing clothes, cooking food, nursing the children, making ready my husband's bed, and working in wool, though, my mother was quick to point out, since my husband was a wealthy man there would be servants to do the most hardy chores. She blessed me for my good fortune to land such a husband. But I could never stop weaving, she said, and I should still bake my own bread.

"Idleness leads to unchastity," she said.

She gave me the doll and pottery animals I played with as a girl, gifts for my future children. She helped me pack my robe, and then she kissed me.

Six months later our wedding took place, though it wasn't the festive occasion it should have been. Normally, the groom arrives at the bride's family home to lead her to his home amidst singing, dancing, and rejoicing. Normally, relatives from all over, friends, and even the entire village would be invited to participate in the celebration. Normally, verses from the sensuous "Song of Songs" would be sung and musicians would play cymbals, harps, lyres, and the shofar to celebrate the union. Normally, the bride is brought in on a litter, her hair on her shoulders, veiled and adorned with jewels, wearing a ceremonial robe embroidered by her mother's hands. When the groom accepted his bride into his home the marriage became official. The groom's father would say a traditional blessing expressing his wishes for the couple's happiness and fruitfulness. The evening would pass in games of counters and dice, sometimes even wrestling and bows and slings, and waves of laughter filled everyone's hearts while the groom danced and the bride withdrew to a room with her brides-maids. The next day, after more rejoicing and dancing, the bridegroom would sing to his bride from the "Song of Songs"...how beautiful thou art, my beloved, how beautiful... and he would praise his new wife's charms. A pomegranate would be crushed, signifying fertility, and a vase filled with erotic scents was broken when the marriage was contracted under the canopy. Normally, there was a feast served, and normally there was a special nuptial chamber where the bride was escorted by her parents. After the couple withdrew to consummate their union, the blood-stained linen was kept as a souvenir because it was said in Deuteronomy that it was proper to have proof against any future allegations of the wife's virginity.

But my wedding didn't have the laughter or the gaiety. It was a somber affair. Othniel bar-Ismael and his two brothers arrived one autumn evening at my home. They were bathed, anointed with aromatic oils, and dressed in their finest cloaks. We ate a festive meal. The dishes were not as elaborate as meals I would later have in Jerusalem, but they were the work of long days of preparation from my mother's own hands and it was the finest feast I ever knew because it was made with her love. It was her wedding gift to me before I moved away, so far from the life she knew in Nazareth. Before the meal, our guests ritually purified themselves by washing their hands from stone water jars. During the meal my new husband's brothers espoused poetry and presented gifts to us, the new couple.

My husband and I left for Jerusalem early the next morning, and, though I was excited at the prospect of living in the great city, as soon as my father's home was out of sight I felt as though I were lacking something. As if I had left something behind.

SEVEN

I hadn't been well. I was dizzy, then nauseous, then starving, then thirsting. My husband hoped it was the beginning of a child, the son he was waiting for, but it wasn't. It was the beginning of my notoriety.

I was nervous all the time and looking over my shoulder. Did he know? Did she know? Why are they looking at me that way? Have they heard something I don't want them to hear? I went to the Court of Women to beg for understanding. Where was El-Shaddai, who promised deliverance? G-d is love, G-d is love, my father said, but I couldn't feel it. Instead, I was distracted by the movements of the men as their shadows danced on the carved stone blocks of the Temple. As the sunlight filtered down, I stared at my feet and thought of the many places I had walked. I had walked through Nazareth, around the hilltops and ravines, and I had walked the twisted, narrow streets of Jerusalem. I had followed my husband home and I had followed the man I loved to places I will not name.

We were alike, my lover and I. We had the same opinions. We held the same things important. I believed if we had met at another time, under other circumstances, we would have loved each other openly and completely. I could dream and try to will it to happen, but I was married to another. I wore my husband's necklace of blood-red stones, and that was the sadness behind my eyes. The man I loved, the man I wanted to wake up next to every morning, was not my husband.

"It's so different talking to you than it is talking to my husband," I said once to my lover.

"How so?" he asked.

"When you and I talk, you listen to me. You're interested in my opinions. You're interested in what I feel. You speak with me, not at me as my husband does. My husband is only interested in putting forth his own ideas. Whatever I say is simply a springboard to his own thoughts. That is when he speaks to me at all because usually he has nothing to say. It's like living with a breathing Roman statue."

I turned away because it was easier to talk about my husband without seeing the face of my lover. When we were together we preferred to forget I was married and we hardly ever spoke of it. Sometimes, though, I was compelled to talk out loud about my husband to remind myself my marriage was real and my love affair wasn't.

My lover was standing across the room from me, his shoulders slumped, his gentle eyes turned down and away, trying to remove himself from the reality of the moment, perhaps afraid of himself and his feelings, afraid to admit what he was thinking. He was in that place where I wanted to follow him if he would let me. He turned the conversation to G-d.

"I want to rise in the Temple," he said to me. "I want to use the ability HaShem has given me. I want to create written works others will read and understand, to bring others closer to the Lord, to help them understand the Law, that is my ultimate goal. This life, its problems and its loves, is fleeting. To do something that lasts forever gives a momentary life meaning."

"You'll do it," I said. "You're already known in Caesaria and Jerusalem for your devotion and learning. You already have the respect of the elders. It won't take much more to make your abilities appreciated by everyone."

"You give me great strength," he said. "It's because of you I'm able to have such far-reaching dreams." He didn't add that because of me his dreams may be left to whither and die because who would listen to a man who was also an adulterer? No one would understand the circumstances that brought us together. People would see the plain-day facts and make assumptions. No one would understand the truth of our hearts. My life would be ruined, I would most certainly die, but he would suffer too. Even if he weren't stoned his career would die, and that would be his end.

"I've seen devotion as great as yours," I said. "My father is a pious man. When I was young he told us stories about how G-d will use you for His purpose if you let Him, about how when Messiah comes it will all be all right. My father loves the story of Abraham. He loves the idea that no matter how old you are, no matter how much you want to take matters into your own hands, if you're patient, if you listen, then you'll learn what the Divine Plan is for you."

He seemed so far, so small, as if he were across the crooked street, standing in the archway of someone else's home. I wondered what he thought of then. He reached into a pocket under his cloak and pulled out a stone, a lapiz lazuli, as blue as the jeweled sky of Nazareth. He put the stone in my hand and kissed my lips.

"I want you to have this," he said. "This stone is permanent, like the sun in the sky. The stones around your neck are inter-connected and keep you bound, but this stone is free. It isn't attached to anything. When you look at this stone I want you to think of me. No matter what happens in the future, we will always have this bond. Whenever you look at this stone I want you to remember that I want you to be free."

I took the stone, and there we were, alone together, he standing, me sitting, not looking at each other but looking into our own hearts, uncomfortable in the moment not because of our feelings but because of what our feelings meant to those around us. Again, I wondered what it would have been like if we had met before, years before, in another time, before the irreparable was done.

MY FATHER WANTED me to have everything I wished for, though he saw clearly what I would not see. He was honest when I was deceived. I thought I would go to Jerusalem where I would become a pampered lady like the ladies I saw in Sepphoris, ladies whose robes cost more than my father earned in a year. I wanted to wear the jewels like the necklace my betrothed had given me. I wanted to wear the plaited hair-styles and eat the gourmet feasts and drink the imported wine. I wanted to spend money without having to sweat for it. I wanted to buy frivolously. I coveted everything the Roman women seemed to have. If I were that rich, I thought, I would be appreciated. I would become important, a person among people. I thought I would be happy. My father shrugged and said he married my mother for love and he wanted me to do the same. He wouldn't force me into a different marriage though it was his right to do so. But I wanted to go to Jerusalem and become a great lady, and I thought I was so fortunate because I, a humble shepherd's daughter, had the opportunity to leave the littleness behind.

In Nazareth, I spent much of my time outdoors. We spent

most of our days outside, in the gleaming sunshine that shimmered broadly over the green hills while white tufts of sheep grazed lazily on the grass. I loved the sparkle of the fresh air and the snap of the south wind on my face. I loved to run my hands through the springy softness of the sheep's wool, and sometimes, when my brother was otherwise occupied I would help my father herd the sheep to place them in their pens for the night. Women in Nazareth went shopping unescorted, chatted with each other easily, warned each other when the tax collector was coming through, and provided places for excesses of grain so that they wouldn't be confiscated by those who wanted but didn't need. I was free in Nazareth, and by the time I realized my freedom was gone it was too late. I was a married woman to a respectable man in Jerusalem, and I was expected to stay within the respectable confines of my walls.

I once asked my husband why he chose me instead of the daughter of a rabbi from the Upper City, someone aristocratic, graceful, and born to good grooming.

"Your bread was the softest I had ever eaten, it melted in my mouth, and it pleased me to think that every day I could eat such bread." He smiled at the memory. "That, and you're beautiful enough to inspire envy in everyone who sees you. I knew you would gain me instant recognition everywhere because people would want to know who the man is with the beautiful wife who bakes bread that tastes of manna from heaven."

And I did love baking bread. Where in Nazareth it was a chore that kept me from grazing with the sheep or daydreaming, in Jerusalem it was the thing that kept me occupied. When I baked bread, my hands rolling the worn stones or kneading the rounds of pliable dough, my mind was focused on the bread and nothing else. My hands were kneading and rolling, prodding and pulling, pounding life into shapeless forms that would rise into sustenance for those who tasted it. Baking bread was to create the essence of life.

I was lonely in Jerusalem. In the Upper City it wasn't so easy for women to congregate in sisterhood as we had in Nazareth, where the women shared common courtyards and assisted each other in births and deaths. In Jerusalem I was restrained, forced to stay inside because whenever I went outside our home, beyond our grounds I got reproving half-stares from the men, only half-stares because it wasn't acceptable for men to look at women on the street. Respectable women were expected to be escorted everywhere and sheltered from inappropriate public exposure. The more wealthy a woman's husband the more secluded her life was.

"It's a sign of prestige," my husband explained, "because it shows that her husband is wealthy enough to hire help or buy slaves to do the busy work. A woman's place is in her home where she can tend her children." His facial expression didn't change when he said this. He didn't grimace or cough. He sniffed, though there were years of frustration in that sound. There were times when the successful Jerusalem textile merchant didn't understand his country wife from the hills of Nazareth, as if he and I were strangers instead of husband and wife. He made no attempt to understand me. He simply wanted what he wanted when he wanted it, and as long everything he wanted was provided he was content. But he wanted an heir, and I hadn't provided one.

"Woman, what have you done wrong?" my husband would ask. "Sterility is a sign of personal sin. How have you sinned?"

He knew how to sting me, my husband. He knew what to say that would bring me the most pain.

Infertility was cause for despair because G-d was the one who opened and closed the womb. If He chose not to open your womb then others wondered what was wrong with you.

Women weren't considered whole if their wombs weren't open because the birth of a child was the most welcome of all events. It meant the continuation of the family through the generations to come. News of the newborn was sent around the village or quarter and the neighbors were told and friends and family were invited to rejoice. Children were a blessing, the highest wealth, though many babies and young children died around us daily. According to the Psalms, a fruitful womb is a reward that comes from Him. But I had no such reward. I tried every remedy I could find. I used folk medicines, went to a priest for purification rites, and visited a physician though doctors were not held high in esteem since only HaShem could heal. I ate pomegranates, symbols of fertility. I drank wild gourd tea, a purgative that was fatal in large doses. But I couldn't conceive. And my husband reminded me frequently.

"Abraham and Sarah were granted Isaac when they were full of years," he said. "I hope we do not have to wait so long."

Every month, after my visit to the mikvah to cleanse myself from my impurities, when I showed no life growing within me, other women shook their heads in shame for me while my husband muttered something I preferred not to hear.

Men complimented me through my husband.

"Your wife keeps Shabbat well."

"Your wife bakes the sweetest bread."

"Your wife is more lovely than a desert flower in the sunlight."

But my husband would be satisfied, he said, when he had a son.

At first, the silences between my husband and me gnawed at my soul. I didn't understand silence. Silence has no vocabulary and made no sense to me. In Nazareth, there was always sound, life noises of children playing, women gossiping, Yosef hammering in the carpenter's shop. The sheep nickered and bayed and occasionally there were the stomping marches of the nuisance Roman soldiers as they monitored the village. The birds chattered overhead in the clear sky, a sky so perfect I thought if I reached my hand up I could touch the Almighty Himself. When I was a girl my father told me stories where he related G-d to a kind, elderly man with a full rabbi's beard who reclined on his left arm, eating grapes with his right hand while he watched the world, His creation, and thinking it was good, and when there was trouble His hand would reach down toward His children, whom He loved, wanting desperately to push them in the direction He meant for them but restraining Himself because He had set the world in motion, He had given everything its proper place and now He could only sit back and watch how it all played out. Now, as a married woman, I wanted a child, and I thought that if I did right, if I said the prayers for Shabbat with passion and prayed silently on my own, if I conducted myself as a pious wife then I would have the desire of my heart—a child of my own, someone I could love and who would love me unconditionally.

Then, as the years passed and no children came, the silence between my husband and me became meditative. I no longer heard the sounds from Nazareth in my head and I could barely remember my girlhood in the sunshine tending the sheep and learning my mother's recipe for bread, watching her rhythmic hands kneading the dough as though she were playing a delicate rounded instrument whose music was filling for the soul. The memories grew more vague, as though they belonged to someone else.

I felt sorry for him sometimes, my husband. I watched him while he sat alone and stared at the scrolls he laid out on the alabaster table in front of him. He meant to study. He meant to be pious, but the daily tasks and concerns of a successful textile merchant who walked in the highest social circles kept his mind occupied while it kept his pouch full. When we were first married I tried to talk to him the way I had talked to my father and brother and uncles and cousins. In Jerusalem some women didn't know how to talk to men, women who hardly spoke to men their entire lives, but in Nazareth, so long as I was not overly bold or put myself into a situation that could be misconstrued, I spoke to whomever I pleased.

But my husband didn't want to talk to me. He quoted the rabbinical saying that a woman shouldn't indulge in serious talk with a man because it brings evil upon the man and he will neglect his study of the Law and inherit GeHennom. I never knew where my husband disappeared to when he pulled into his silence. In my silences I struggled to see Nazareth again, the place I couldn't wait to leave. I remembered my girlhood dreams of the kind of man I would marry. I thought he would be handsome, kind, generous, and pious, like my father. I thought he would be scholarly and open. I thought his love for HaShem would be first and foremost in his heart, and I thought his eyes would catch me the moment I looked at him. I thought when he saw me he would love me as I would love him. In my perfect dreams for my perfect life I wanted someone to love me as much as I could love in return, which was much.

In Nazareth, there were constant chores. For my father and brother there were prayers and studies, and for my mother and me there was Shabbat and the holidays to prepare for. Those were the best days, the holidays. Even the most oppressed among us, those hit hardest by taxes and a poor yield of crops, would smile, dance, and sing during the holidays, allowing ourselves this time to worship G-d who gives us air to breathe, food to eat, and people to love. I thought about everyone I knew in Nazareth, my large family of aunts, uncles, and cousins. I thought of my father, his respectability as a village elder, his kindness and generosity, his joy for life.

In Jerusalem, there was comfort in keeping my hands busy with daily tasks—baking bread, weaving, keeping my husband's prayer shawl in pristine condition so it was pure white and true blue, the tzitzit long and well-kept. I stayed busy to stay sane. In Nazareth, I could leave my home, wander the village, breathe the clean air that filtered over from the Sea of Galilee and walk with my feet brushing the edge of the riverbank, cooling me from the hot-filled sunlight that passed unadorned over the desert. In Jerusalem, it was crowded and I didn't like the crowds. I didn't like having to elbow my way through dark, narrow, winding streets to the markets or push my way through the Temple gates, and I didn't like the sideway glances from other women when I was out unescorted. If I left the house for air and sunlight I had to walk where I wouldn't be seen much, as if there were such a place in that walled city where everyone knew everyone else. People knew you were the rabbi or the rabbi's wife, or the tax collector, or the nephew of the high priest, or the woman of ill repute, everyone knew everything about you. But in Nazareth there was community. In Jerusalem, there were prying eyes and pointing fingers hiding behind cloaks and prayer shawls. There was nowhere to hide.

When I first looked upon Jerusalem, it seemed to me a city of stones, as though the mountains and hills were giant rocks and someone had carved a city from it, the homes, the gates, the open courts of the wealthy, and the Temple of gilded stone. At times I thought it was the home of a G-d of stone who watched the suffering of the beggars, the ill, and the poverty-stricken, passing along a few shekels at a time, providing just enough so the beggars wouldn't die that day. Who else but a G-d of stone could listen to the helpless, piteous cries of

"Unclean! Unclean!" of the lepers outside the city gates, their scarred, bleeding hands skeleton-like, sometimes fingerless, sometimes handless stumps, pleading, we need to eat, too, though we are different than you.

Our holy men instructed us to help the poor, the widows, the orphans, and the lepers, and yet... These human wrecks had plaintive voices painful to hear and appearances hard to see, the men and women with white nodular patches eating their skin off their bones, a lion's mask on their faces. Most who heard their cries couldn't bear to look at them for fear of having to face the ugliness. It was so easy to become ill in Jerusalem. It was too hot in the day and freezing in the night, and the number of deaths escalated during the months of the east winds. There was dysentery from the hot weather and frequent blindness caused by the arid climate and the harsh light, the wind, and the dust. There was arthritis, parasites, lice, whipworm, rodents, tuberculosis, flies, septic infections, polluted water, poor hygiene, trauma, and mutilations. Many people began well but became ill, the priests said, because of sins—either their sins or the sins of their family. The priests said there was no cure for these sad people. G-d alone could cure them, if He chose.

"The wages of sin is death," the rabbis said.

We were beckoned to give alms—you must help those who cannot help themselves. Yet those who couldn't help themselves were "Unclean! Unclean!" and to come too close to them, especially to touch them, meant you became "Unclean! Unclean!" too. Kind people and family members would throw whatever coins or crumbs they could spare to these pathetic beings through the city gates for fear of being touched by one of them. But the rabbis insisted many of them had sinned and therefore had brought such maladies upon themselves. I heard the cries in my twisted dreams, "Unclean! Unclean!" and my heart broke for them. When I thought I wouldn't be seen I threw shekels to the beggars through the city gates and they would jump on the coins and shout blessings at me.

Do not bless me, I would think in my shame. I throw shekels at you as though you are rabid dogs, afraid of being seen doing this small act of charity, afraid of my husband knowing. Under the law I was unable to donate to charity without my husband's permission because if he objected then the alms were considered theft. I'm just like you, I would think, only I'm on this side of the gate and you are there. I could be on your side, ostracized, alone. We are all sinners after all.

"G-d is a G-d of love," I heard my father say. He told me how El-Shaddai provided for everyone, even those who seemed unloved. G-d loves us all, my father said.

"If anyone should come to your door," my father said, "you may not turn him away empty handed. You must give whatever you can give, even a morsel of bread. You may not rebuke or speak harshly to the poor for their hearts are broken and their spirits downcast. We must be like parents to the poor and show them mercy in words, in deeds, and when giving alms," my father said, "do it with a good heart. Do not boast of one's deeds when helping the poor, the infirm, the orphaned, or the widowed."

Women were especially called to show hospitality, my father told me. Women were to follow the example of pious mother Sarah. Women should be especially kind to strangers and offer food even if they don't ask because the stranger may be too ashamed to say he's hungry.

"If you have, share," my father said, "for when you need you will want others to share with you. When you consider others before yourself you glorify G-d."

"If HaShem has made sure that we are provided for then why are there still poor and needy in the world, abba?" I asked.

"Because people do not heed His will," my father said. "The problem isn't with G-d. The problem is with us. People die of hunger because of hearts of stone. And people die of loneliness because others turn their backs on them."

I asked my father the question again when we saw a blind old man sitting lonely near the village gate, his withered, weathered hand outstretched for any spare taste of bread. We went home and my father and I returned with a loaf, half of our family's daily share.

"Where is He here?" I asked.

"G-d is in the heart of those who love this man," my father answered. "G-d is in you. You will understand, one day. Now you do not believe because you think G-d is out of the ordinary. But G-d is here," he pointed to my head, "and here," pointing to my heart.

On the days when I walked the Jerusalem roads I would take Nima, my girl servant, and step my way around the back streets, looking for some fragment of nature to hold onto. The city was ugly to me. The glamour I was so sure I would find wasn't there. Jerusalem was the holiest of all cities, yet I felt no connection to the Almighty there. The only moments of understanding I had ever felt with Him were when I ran through the Nazareth grass, the wind in my hair, when I stopped to pick wildflowers, making sage-colored grass chains for my parents to wear. In Jerusalem, I rarely left through the city gates though I longed to. I thought there might be some freedom past the gates but there was also terror. Along the western road was Golgotha, the place of the skull, a disfigured, abandoned quarry where the mountain hovered like a mask of death, where criminals were executed in the most grotesque of ways, where men, women—Jews—were hung on a tree, the epitome of disgrace to a Jew as it says in Deuteronomy, and left to die in breathless, pain-filled terror. Traitors, the Romans called them. Enemies of Rome. The sight was gruesome, bloody, unbearable. I passed a mass crucifixion once and vowed never to make that mistake again.

Inside Jerusalem I looked for open spaces but found none. I looked up at the blue sky, the same sky that covered Nazareth, and I closed my eyes and dreamed I was home listening to my father's stories about people more pious than me.

I remember the morning when Nima and I walked the crowded streets toward the marketplace, our woven baskets dangling from our swinging arms. As we drew closer I pulled my basket closer to me as the crowds became unruly. I heard the shouts of the people haggling with the vendors along with the clopping of camel hooves on streets barely wide enough for them to pass. Crowds of pilgrims and worshippers hustled toward the Temple while the women bought grain for bread or textiles for weaving or meat for Shabbat. I needed to make a few purchases so I could prepare a proper meal to keep the Sabbath holy. Some women who lived near me in the Upper City had their servant girls take care of their purchases, but I preferred to go myself to the marketplace. I enjoyed going with Nima, though she rarely spoke. My husband acquired the girl when her father failed to pay a debt he owed my husband. My husband thought he had handled the situation well. Rather than take the poor man's cloak, as he was entitled to, he took the man's daughter instead. The man seemed relieved.

"You can have her," the man said. "Already she's two years past marriageable age."

Nima was agreeable and gentle, always ready to do my bidding before I thought to ask. She was a silent participant in our home. She knew when to wash the linens in floral-scented water. She helped me bake bread for feast days and she helped care for my husband's mother when she was being difficult, which was often. With Nima nearby I could walk the streets without being bothered by the pointing fingers or whispering lips of others.

That morning, as Nima and I neared the marketplace, there was a horrific sounding commotion across the way. The stone-built walls echoed a woman's scream and the shouts of men complemented her anguish. As the stomping and yelling grew nearer, I grabbed Nima's hand and she clutched mine. A group of 10 strong men had a young woman by the arms, dragging her toward the gate that led out of Jerusalem, toward Golgotha. The people in the marketplace went about their business as though nothing were out of the ordinary. Finally, one man dared to shout, "What is her crime?"

One of the men marching the girl out of the city answered, "She disobeys HaShem. Curses on her mother!"

My heart sank. The young woman's screams were like bloodletting, but her face was defiant. She struggled against the men who dragged her and she spat on them and tried to scratch them and kick them away. But she was too small and they were too big and she fought until she was breathless. Nima and I held hands as the violent procession passed. I grabbed a woman, her head in her hands, weeping as though mourning the dead. The woman read my question in my eyes.

"She will be stoned," the woman said.

And then I saw them. Stones bigger than the men's fists, stones they had to carry with both hands because the weight was so great. A young man dropped his stone on his foot and he fell behind the crowd as they dragged the girl past the city gate and beyond my vision. The crowd dwindled away, and the Roman centurions who had been looking on with curious smiles left to find other entertainment. Only Nima and I remained. When they were a proper distance from the city gate the frenzied crowd would stone that young woman to death. I heard about games the Romans played, games where human lives were destroyed for the sport of it, blood spilled in laughter and gaiety. The Romans lived a lifestyle based on violence—battles, domination, and gladiator games. Violence, not an emperor, was their king. For Romans, violence was an escape from daily reality, the chance to watch someone else suffering. I wasn't convinced that these stonings were anything different.

"Will no one help her?" I asked aloud. But no one heard me. "Is this G-d's will?" But I knew how the men would answer. She disobeyed the Law, they would say. They would quote Deuteronomy, and they would point out the rabbis' teachings about those lines in Deuteronomy, and they would explain, as though I were an imbecile, why it was a crime against G-d when a married woman committed adultery. Adultery from a man was simply a man being a man. Adultery from a woman meant the family lineage was no longer sacred. Adultery from the woman meant the paternal origins of offspring would always be questioned. Adultery from the woman meant no one could ever be sure who the fathers were, and since fathers signified family, then families were no longer pure.

To not know the identity of your father meant the law of primogeniture, passing down property and wealth to the first-born son, was no longer accurate. If a man passed down his property to a son who was not the offspring of his seed, it meant his family could be erased from the face of the earth, their family name never again written in the Book of Life. Along with barrenness, that was one of the worst things that could happen to a people who believed in a G-d who commanded "Go forth and multiply."

Nima disappeared into the marketplace, but I remained, watching the light fading through the arch of the gate. I could see the skull, the hill of Golgotha, the place of execution, and I knew the poor girl was probably being stoned as I stood there. Will no one help her? I thought again, contemplating the stones and how the men would be hurling them toward her with all their strength. Stoning wasn't done frequently, but it was always there, pointing stone-stub fingers toward the women who might fall. Do wrong and we are there, the stones said. We are everywhere. Look down at your feet and see countless of our numbers ready to expedite your end. After all, Jerusalem was a city of stones. Everything—stairs, homes, the Temple—was stone. The roads beneath our feet were paved with stone. The utensils we used in our homes, to cook, to weave, to live, were stone. Everything was stone.

Finally, the sun set pink-red in the sky and the skull on the hill cast a demon shadow on the ground. The gatekeepers would soon shut the gates for the night and no one would be allowed in or out of the city until dawn. The girl's family, her executioners and those who went to watch the spectacle, would return soon or else be locked out overnight. They would return without the girl, without the harlot, the sinner. I wondered if she had loved the man, if she went to her death willingly for the opportunity to be loved. I wondered if she had children or if she had ever loved her husband. I stood there until Nima led me by the arm toward the Temple where my husband waited for me.

At the Temple I sidestepped the priests as they rushed through the Temple gates, late for a ceremony, arriving for a sacrifice, running toward the tithes. How many women had I heard whisper "Is this all there is?" during their prayers in the Women's Court? How many women had I seen sway themselves, back and forth, eyes closed tightly, back and forth, concentrating on G-d and His mercy and needing some reprieve from their hard lives, back and forth. They opened their eyes, saw the men praying fervently below, back and forth, wearing the prayer shawls with the ground-length fringes we women couldn't wear. We weren't holy enough, the men said, not clean enough to wear the garments of El-Shaddai. The women opened their eyes from their prayers and saw themselves in the same Temple, in the same street, with the same rags on their bodies and the same worn sandals on their calloused feet. They saw the blood of the sacrificed, blood meant to cleanse the way toward something better. Some, like me, cringed at the screams of the animals. Others were too lost in the thought that their sins, whatever they had done wrong to deserve this life, were washed away and now they could start again, and again, and again when the cleansing didn't work the other times.

"I'm late, my lord," I said to my husband as I approached him outside the Nicanor Gate. I tried not to stutter as I spoke. "I was at the marketplace and a girl was being dragged out to be stoned."

"I am aware of that," my husband said. He looked at the rabbi standing to his right and nodded. "She is a blatant adulteress who has broken the Lord's commandment. An adulterous wife is worse than a shrew, and there's nothing else to do with a whore like that, may her name be erased."

"The crime of adultery is ranked with the supreme crime of atheism," the rabbi said. "Job described how adulterers wait for nightfall, saying within themselves, 'No one sees me' when G-d Almighty sees all. It is impossible to do anything that He does not know. And then the sinner must suffer for the sins. It is the Law."

"Not all wives are industrious," my husband said. "Many are unpleasant, stupid, or disobedient."

Jeremiah the Scribe joined the two men. "Not all husbands are kind," he said.

"Husbands do not have to be kind," my husband said.

Several men from the Temple joined my husband as he walked home. I trailed behind them, vaguely hearing their laughter while still thinking about the young woman who had been dragged through the city gates. I saw her matted hair, her skin burned raw as it scraped against the road, the stones carried by the men. I saw her kohl-lined eyes and her dangling earrings, dressed as alluringly as a prostitute, as Tamar must have looked when she seduced Judah to secure her livelihood.

Is she dead now? I wondered. Are they still stoning her, still crushing her breath from her and making her bleed until she's dried and shriveled inside? I shuddered and tried to follow the conversation of the men as they walked before me. I shuddered again when I glanced over my veil at Jeremiah the Scribe, and I shuddered more when he returned my gaze.

EIGHT

$\mathcal{M}$ y husband spent his mornings in prayer, head bowed, the ritual fringes on his prayer shawl narrowly missing the floor. He made sure I took care with his shawl. He watched me wash it, press it, and tend to the fringes on the four corners, just as the Almighty decreed.

"It must look perfect," my husband said. "When I am in the Temple the high priest may be watching."

My husband was adamant that no one disturb him during the first hours after the sunrise. No matter who, he told me, even if it was the high priest, he must be turned away so that my husband could concentrate on G-d.

When Caiaphas, the high priest himself, arrived at our door early one morning I turned him away. "My husband is in prayer," I said, "and he cannot be disturbed." When he learned of it, my husband became fierce.

"Woman, you are useless! How could you turn the high priest away? The most revered man at the Temple!" My husband called me a fool and himself a bigger fool for thinking a simple girl from Nazareth would ever be useful no matter how wide her smile or how sweet her bread.

My bread was all I had. I took pride in the smack of people's lips as they tasted my bread. It was no simple task to impress the Jerusalem elite, though I hadn't set out to impress anyone. I merely adhered to my mother's teachings that feeding someone, both stomach and soul, is one of the greatest gifts we can give. I remembered watching my mother's weathered hands knead the dough. She pulled the dough, formed it into a circle, then stretched it again, shaping it into something pleasing to both the eye and the mouth. She learned the recipe from her mother, who learned it from her mother, who learned it from her mother, from far back women have been nourishing their families.

One morning I was kneading the dough and adding the sour-smelling yeast when my husband's manservant came to me.

"He is here again, madam," the servant said. "Caiaphas, the high priest. He is here, but the master cannot be disturbed. What shall I tell him?"

I dusted the flour from my hands and went to meet the important man. When I walked into the front room, where Caiaphas stood, I noticed that his eyes, small, black, and barely visible from beneath his head cover, were intent on me. I bowed my head. If he weren't the high priest I would have found lewdness in his looks.

"I am here to see your husband," he said.

"Of course," I said. "This way please."

The high priest glanced at my hands. I looked at my hands, too, studying their creases and my ridged nails, wondering if they looked like my mother's, wrinkled and careworn. Caiaphas brushed past me toward my husband's room.

"I know the way," he said. "I'll show myself."

Caiaphas disappeared behind the curtain where my husband prayed. I heard quiet whisperings, melodies of secrets and lies. Once my husband poked his head around the curtain and startled me with his impatient glare. I turned toward the outside door with dough in my hands, ready for the stone oven that would bring the bread to life, expanding it like a breathing chest, bringing warmth to everyone around. I ran toward the oven to get away from my husband's gaze.

"She's from Nazareth," I heard him say as he pulled his head back behind the curtain.

A short time later the two men left for the Temple, both stopping once more to cast furtive glances my way. Caiaphas stepped close to me.

"You are from Nazareth?" he asked.

"Yes, sir," I answered.

Caiaphas nodded. When the men left I felt cold though it was hot outside and I should have been sweltering from the heat. But even beneath the sunshine I shivered. I put a shawl around my shoulders and sat under an olive tree, trying to warm myself but not succeeding. I sat there the rest of the afternoon, until after sundown. When my husband returned he had a gift for me: a Jerusalem of Gold.

Later that night, at the Temple, I scanned the shapes of the people, searching out his tall, lurching figure. Knowing he was there, somewhere close, was enough. I could see him in my mind's eye and that would settle me, for that moment, at least.

Finally, I heard him, his voice hovering above the cacophony of Temple sounds. He hummed when he walked and sometimes, in a happier mood, he whistled. He walked hunched, his back a widow's hump, an apology for his height. When he straightened he stood a head taller than the men around him. When you talked to him he leaned close and made eye contact, talking to you as if you were the only person there, making you feel as though he understood exactly what you were feeling, he has been where you have been.

But the painful part wasn't my fascination with a man who could never be mine. I was used to the dull longing, the gnawing need for something else, the lack of contentment and understanding. I felt it at the Temple in prayer. I felt it when I was alone with my husband and we were silent with each other. The only time I didn't feel it was when I was baking bread because then my hands were busy twisting, turning, and pushing life into the dough. There was a mystery to the bread as it changed shape before me. Baking bread was the only peace I knew. When I baked too much, which I often did, I brought the extra to the city gates and threw large chunks to the gnarled beggars outside or I passed whole loaves into the sad hands of a blind, childless widow and she would try to grab my hands and kiss them. When the beggars touched me before I could pull away, I went home and washed in water so hot my skin burned. I would bandage my hands and tell my husband I had scorched myself on the bread oven, the stones were hotter than I thought, and he didn't question me. I should have seen a rabbi to have the ritual cleansing prayers said over me, but I couldn't risk someone telling my husband where the burns had truly come from because then he would prohibit me from bringing bread to the hungry. Once, when my husband and I were first married, I made extra bread to feed the hungry as my mother had always done in Nazareth. He was furious, telling me I was wasting flour.

"It's such a small amount of flour," I said, "though it can do much good for those who have none."

My husband responded with a tirade about why we shouldn't worry about the hungry.

"They have sinned," he said. "They must have done things so terrible that the Almighty decided that living without the necessities was punishment for their sins. And who are we to decide the Almighty is wrong about these things? If they were G-d fearing people, if they lived according to the laws of Moses, they wouldn't be where they are now. They would be in their comfortable homes eating bread and drinking wine as we do. They would have guardian angels like all who observe the Law. Besides, the Law allows them to take ears of overlooked corn from the fields and fallen bunches of grapes from the vineyard. They won't starve to death."

I LEARNED it was my laughter that brought me to his attention as more than just his acquaintance's wife. In Nazareth, women were loud in their joy. We were poor and lived hard but we found miracles around us every day and we weren't shy about expressing happiness. Women from Jerusalem would call us coarse or loud, but we were happy. In Jerusalem, women smiled politely and laughed silently only in the company of other women. This was a conservative society where joy was considered too light for the pious. I wasn't from Jerusalem, not so conservative, and laughter held no fear for me. The first time he had come to dine with my husband I laughed at something the rabbi said, and his head snapped around to see who had laughed.

Perhaps that was why I felt so drawn to him despite everything else. He was the only man, besides my father, who spoke to me as if I had something to offer. He was the only person I could talk to about religion, politics, everything I wasn't supposed to concern myself with. I was supposed to care for my husband's home, and I did care for my husband's home. I loved baking the bread that nourished the company that frequented our table, and I longed for the day when I would have children to bind to me with never-ending heartstrings.

But I had thoughts, too, intelligent thoughts, even, and I couldn't talk about them with anyone but my lover. He didn't keep a prudent silence with me as other men would. When I listened in during the men's conversations at the table, he was my voice. He said what I would have said if I were able to share my ideas. He didn't become angry or impatient as the other men did. He didn't raise his voice against anyone. Often, he was the one who made a point of patience and humility, the one who begged forgiveness for others and understanding for everyone. He reminded me of my father. He had a good heart. He knew how to make others feel they were important and that what they had to say was worthwhile. I thought he could show me what my father always meant for me to know—that G-d is a G-d of love.

When he came to visit my husband and my husband wasn't home, I would tell him what I thought of the conversation he was involved in during his last visit. He didn't laugh at me or think I sounded like a man. He sat, one long leg crossed over another, his torso leaning back into the couch, his eyes piercing into mine, and he explained why he said what he said, what he wanted to say, why he thought the others were wrong. He was fascinated by my stories of my life in Nazareth. He asked questions about my father and my mother. He was an aristocratic scribe from the coastal city of Caesarea, Herod's largest and busiest port where profiteers exported the riches of the east to Rome. Herod built the Hellenized city in the style of the great gentile cities he had known, and there were pagan temples surrounded by ornate columns and forbidden idols in the form of statues of their pagan gods. Important Jews took Greek names, spoke Greek and Latin, read Greek philosophy and poetry, and where magnificent public structures like the theater and the stadium stood tall.

"Why did you come to Jerusalem?" I asked him once.

"Because I wanted to be around Jews who know they're Jews, Jews who follow the Torah, worship at the Temple, and know G-d is holy."

"Is that what you found here?" I asked.

He shook his head as he considered his words. "I'm not fond of what I've found in Jerusalem. I came here with Psalm 48 ringing a sublime melody in my head: 'Walk about Zion, go round about her, number her towers, consider well her ramparts, go through her citadels, that you may tell the next generation that this is G-d, our G-d for ever and ever...' But what I find instead is hypocrisy."

He plucked the hairs on his beard, his eyes downcast, his mind elsewhere. Suddenly, I wondered if his beard was as soft as it looked, and I wondered what it would feel like to touch it. I liked the way his shoulders shrugged when he laughed.

And then we began. Cautiously. So no one would know.

We had to stay out of the prying eyes of the pious, a difficult task. As far as anyone knew, we believed, we had never said anything in front of others that went beyond proper social conduct, had never touched each other, had never looked at each other openly, had never been seen speaking to each other. A man couldn't be seen talking to a woman without inciting gossip, and what was worse was, in this case, the gossip would have been true.

Did I feel guilty about betraying my husband? Sometimes. My husband wasn't warm or loving. He wasn't comfortable or soft, though he treated me well in his way. My husband and I spent weeks without talking about more than the profitability of his business, the rising price of wool, the difficulties of finding weavers who would work for the low wages he wanted to pay them, the number of men he was having to our home to break bread that day. The day to day existence between us was a formality. He didn't tell me the specifics of his day, and I didn't tell him mine. We went to Temple several times a week, and we walked together, he several steps ahead while I trailed dutifully behind, and people nodded at us, the pious couple going to worship together, he a noted friend of the priests and scribes, and me, his helpmeet who supported him in his pursuits of business and piety.

But my lover wanted to know me. He wanted to know how I spent my days. Often he followed me into the courtyard while I checked the baking bread, making sure it cooked long enough for the crust to crunch but not so long that the spongy inside would dry out. Some mornings we went to the court-yard or onto the roof and watched the sun rise higher over the city of gold, illuminating the Temple in the distance and the vendors outside the Temple gates. If you breathed silently you could hear the voices of the moneychangers and the animal sellers as they set their tables up around the courts, ready for profit.

One day I nearly left the city through the gate that led toward the place of the skull. I pulled my shawl over my head to protect myself from the heat of the brittle sun and walked down the western road. I was looking for something, a quiet place to think, a way out, the road back to Nazareth, perhaps, where I could go back through the years and become the young girl I was before my husband came through looking for a shepherd with whom to do business. I wanted to go back through the years to find a young man, before he was a widower, who wanted to praise G-d daily and live according to His teachings. That young man and my young self would fall into each other's arms, get married, and live long years together.

As I walked I tripped over the fist-sized stones, falling several times and scraping my calves and palms. Suddenly, I stumbled into Golgotha and saw the men hanging from trees.

The moans, the wails, some from the victims, some from their families as they stayed nearby, were too much. I retched into the sand beneath my feet, and I crawled onto my knees, waiting for the city walls to stop crumbling around me. Finally, I picked myself up and wandered back, thinking about the tortured, their families, the woman I had seen dragged past the city gates to that very spot, wondering how long it had taken her to die. When I arrived home, I told my husband I wasn't well and I stretched out behind the netting, dreaming of the life I meant to live but missed.

I became paranoid and saw stonings and crucifixions in my sleep. Awake and asleep my conscience was on fire and my soul suffered. Everywhere I looked I saw staring faces, disappointed eyes, poking fingers, whispered misunderstandings. I wanted to run away with him, go somewhere, anywhere. I wanted to disappear with Lilith and Vashti, though I wouldn't disappear alone but with the man I loved. I began to hide in my home. I became afraid of the men my husband had over to break bread. But still I met with him, still I loved him, so my paranoia grew even more.

The only time I wasn't afraid was when I was with him. I sought him out more frequently. I watched my husband for signs that he knew, but he didn't show anything I couldn't account for. I wanted to divorce my husband and be free from the suspicion and the fear of being found out. But divorce wasn't an option for me. The choice for divorce belonged solely to my husband. My only choice was to make myself so disagreeable that my husband would take the initiative and divorce me, but that tactic didn't often work in the woman's favor. The rabbis allowed the man to repudiate his wife even when the problems with the marriage were his—impotence, refusal to carry out matrimonial duties, habitual cruelty, incurable diseases like leprosy, the adoption of a disgusting kind of work like collecting dog dung for tanners, or the decision to leave Palestine and live far away. There were reasons my husband might divorce me when the fault was my own. Adultery was one cause for divorce, and sending an unfaithful wife to her death was a husband's legal option. Not all betrayed husbands sent their wives to death. Some publicly denounced their wives while others sent their wives quietly away. Husbands could be rid of their wives without granting her a get, a writ of separation. If a wife had the "taint of defilement" whether the charges were true or not her husband could cast her out. If she had no family who would take her in she was left to fend for herself. If she was repugnant or disagreeable, a bad cook, if she was sterile for ten years or more then her husband could be rid of her. Women were bound to men for their shelter and sustenance, and men reminded women of it daily.

I didn't love my husband. I loved another. What was I to do?

NINE

*S*he looked at me as though she were trying to be kind, but there was a hidden smile within her. She was my sister-in-law, my brother's wife. My brother moved to Jerusalem shortly after I arrived since he wanted to learn about my husband's work. Instead of becoming a textile merchant, however, my brother made a success of spice importing. He wanted to live in Jerusalem, my brother, live in the luxury he had witnessed in Sepphoris, as I had, so he married the daughter of one of my husband's wealthy associates. I was visiting my sister-in-law as family obligation said I should, though seeing my brother always brought me pain. I couldn't help but think of my old father in Nazareth tending the sheep alone, telling Bible stories only to my mother and himself.

My brother and his family lived close to us in the Upper City. With my husband's help, my brother was rising in Jerusalem society. My sister-in-law was the very picture I saw in my mind's eye when my husband first entranced me with visions of Jerusalem. She had high-piled, plaited hair that was illegal to undo on Shabbat because it required work. Her tunic pins were gold. She wore bracelets of exotic beads from the East. She kept her neck outstretched to show off her Jerusalem of Gold. She was respected and pampered, which is what I had meant to be.

"You must be careful," she said when we were alone, her voice implying a whisper. "You've been seen. People are talking." She spoke as if I had been sharing the shadows of my secrets with her.

I looked at the red wine flat in my glass, my own private river, like Pharaoh's Nile flooded with blood. "I don't understand," I said.

I realize now I never knew my sister-in-law well. She and I often visited the mikvah near the southern steps of the Temple Mount together, our ritual purification after our monthly uncleanliness. I thought we had bonded during our total immersions under the water when we pronounced the benediction thanking Him for bidding us to observe the ceremony of immersion. But now, in her home, she was a stranger, as if she were no more than the mikvah attendant, the woman who helped us submerge ourselves so that not even a strand of hair remained above water, the woman who wouldn't look at us though we stood naked before her. We were always unclean, women, always menstruating, getting married, having relations with our husbands, giving birth, handling dead bodies, and becoming ill. There was always a reason for us to isolate ourselves, cleanse ourselves, and immerse ourselves. The men believed we were so unclean we could contaminate a cushion by sitting on it, a bed by laying on it, or a man by touching him.

It was close to the hour when the day would disappear, and my sister-in-law nodded at the young servant girl who went about the room lighting the flax wicks in the ceramic lamps in niches in the walls. As the olive oil lamps grew bright, I believed the shadows were watching me, taking note of my movements. I thought I had drunk too much of the unwatered wine from her father's vineyard. I needed to be home before sundown, but I felt lightheaded and didn't move. I looked at the window high in the wall and felt certain there were spies were peering at me, taking note of me, reading past my stone-like demeanor and understanding what lay inside my heart.

Sitting in my sister-in-law's home, drinking her wine, listening to the joyful noise of her two young sons playing ball outside, I thought of the Commandments and I was afraid. If she knew, then it was commonly known. But perhaps she didn't mean what I thought she meant. Perhaps I misunderstood her. After all, she didn't turn me out of her home. She didn't cry "Sinner!" or "Adulteress!" or "Unclean!" and send me away in shame.

"Everyone is talking about that teacher from Nazareth." She sat beside me sipping wine. "The miracles they say he does! As if anyone could believe a carpenter from Nazareth could be Messiah." Her eyes sparkled with mischief. "Forgive me, Sister. I forgot you're from Nazareth. Did you know the carpenter? Your brother says he wasn't familiar with him."

"I saw him leaning over the sawhorse crafting a door or a wheel. I saw him around the village installing locks or shutters. But I can't say I knew him."

My sister-in-law placed a bowl of pistachios and almonds in front of me. "They say he gathers crowds," she said. "That's what scares the men. The crowds. My husband says the Sanhedrin has been devious, devising a way to capture him. They believe they'll prove him blasphemous when he arrives in Jerusalem. They say he's already heading this way."

I nodded, unsurprised. My husband had told me that news already. Struggling to keep a steady hand, I drank my wine before it taunted me.

TEN

J bent over my knees, heaving and gasping in the center of the Court with only the fading day to witness my shame. I was alone, only the fist-sized stones remaining, mocking me. I wept. I screamed. I shook myself frenzied, still in the Temple where I was branded the woman of stones—a sinner. I felt the tempest rushing through me as if I were an outlet for the storms of all malcontent. I sat on my heels and my feet went numb. I pressed my hands together so tightly my blood couldn't reach my fingers, an act of prayer begging for forgiveness. I felt the stifling pain but I wouldn't move. I was alone in the world, I thought. All alone in the Temple Court while the taunts of the stones echoed in my head.

I don't know how long I sat there, terrified, then relieved, then sorrowful, then repentant. I had been caught, as the rabbis gloated to the teacher, in the very act of adultery. I was going to die. There was no defense for me since it was all true and the Law was the Law. I would have told them myself—it was all true. I would have told them because I was tired of looking over my shoulder and wondering what people's passing glances meant. I was paranoid at every shuffle. And then my sin was released and I was free. I would die because I deserved to die. I would suffer as I deserved to suffer. Instead I was saved.

I staggered to my feet and stumbled at every step. My body felt light, silly, as if my blood had drained from me in preparation for the stoning. Where to go? I didn't know. I had nowhere. I no longer belonged anywhere or to anyone. I couldn't go back to my home in the Upper City. I couldn't show my face to anyone.

"She is the one," I could hear them say. "She is the one who sinned."

I could have walked back to Nazareth, but in my shame I didn't think my mother would have me. I spent two days hiding in the garden at Gethsemane, sleeping behind the gnarled olive trees, looking down at the city of Jerusalem, wondering when they would find me, killing stones in hand, for surely they would come back for me. Forgiveness of that magnitude cannot last longer than anger, I thought. Surely the frustration would rise again and require the men to pick up the stones they dropped, and they would come to find me. But two days turned to three days, and still there was no one. I stayed hidden, thirsting and hungry, until the fourth morning when I crawled out from the brambles and stood, trembling and stretching myself toward the sky.

What would I do? Where could I go? I didn't know. I still wanted to go home to Nazareth, but I was certain I would be stoned along the way. I realized I had nowhere else to go but to my brother's. He was the only family I had in Jerusalem now that my husband had publicly denounced me. And if for no other reason than loyalty to our father, I believed my brother would take me in.

I was wrong. The brother of my girlhood, my partner in childhood, knew of my crime, as everyone in Jerusalem knew of my crime. The wife of Othniel bar-Ismael, the childless, barren woman, the woman who had been taken from the nowhere of Nazareth and made a fine lady in Jerusalem, she has made a cuckold of her husband, a good man, a respected man, a pious man who breaks bread with the high priest himself.

I arrived at my brother's home to be turned away by the servant.

"My master is very angry," the servant said, the judgment against me blazing in his eyes. "He doesn't want you here. He has rented his clothes and declared you dead. He no longer has a sister."

"But what am I to do?" I pleaded.

The servant slammed the door in my face.

I slumped behind my brother's house, my veil held tight beneath my eyes so no one would recognize me. In my fear-crazed mind I remembered when I had gone back to Nazareth the year before, a respectable married woman, a woman with a husband with important social connections. I made quite a scene in my village as I walked down the main road, past the simple homes. My husband thrived on the attention. He threw coins, silver denarii, the ones with the name Tiberius on one side and a seated female figure with the words High Priest on the other. The children raced for the coins, thinking this man was an agent of G-d. Some parents even fought their own children because this money could alleviate the tax crunch soon to come. We arrived at my father's home amidst a crowd that looked like a Roman pageant. My mother opened her door to see my husband and me surrounded by many villagers and she cried. Later my mother told me of the prophetic vision she had when she first saw me standing in the street. She saw me amid a crowd at another time in another way. She saw how my life would change drastically in one moment of posterity.

I had returned to Nazareth with my husband to help my mother care for my father. By the time I arrived my much-loved father had already died, so I helped my mother prepare his body for a ceremonial funeral instead. When my father was dying my mother was forbidden to touch or move him in case his death should be hastened. My mother was forbidden from doing anything about the funeral before my father's death, forbidden from preparing the shrouds. When she answered the door and I saw her rented shawl, rented just as Jacob rented his garment when he learned Joseph's coat was found in tatters and stained with blood, I knew I was too late. My father was gathered to his people.

Since my husband created a partnership with my father, my father prospered and he no longer slept on a rush mat but on a bed. My cousin left the room, and I watched my father sleep the sleep of death. My sorrow was stunted, a bland depression. I looked at my father lying out on the bed in the dark room, and I wondered if he knew that I had come from Jerusalem for one more moment with him.

Are you here, now, El-Shaddai? I wondered, alone in the dark room with my dead father. My father spent his life in awe of you, our G-d is an awesome G-d, he said so many times. My mother said he died with prayers on his lips. Are you here at the moment of death, El-Shaddai, when we no longer need your help in any earthly way? Do you understand our fears, our longings, our need to love and be loved while we are alive? Where are you now, this G-d of love my father lived and died by? I thought of the line from my father's favorite psalm—Be still and know that I am G-d. But it was no comfort to me.

My father's greatest dream was not for his life but for his death. He dreamed of being buried in the Kidron Valley in Jerusalem in the famous cemetery of Jehoshaphat, where every believing Jew longed to be buried. My mother had already decided that, in one year, after my father's bones were reburied in an ossuary, he would receive his desire and I would live close to my father again. Though I was in pain from his loss I thought back over his teachings, how he believed life on earth was merely preparation, and a hard one, for the hereafter where all would be right. My father accumulated more than his share of good deeds, and his rewards in the hereafter would be great. He would receive his rewards.

"Daughter," he told me once, "we have souls, and our souls are our very portions of the Almighty. Our souls are our gifts from Him so we might do his bidding on earth. And for the soul life begins anew after the body's death. After death the soul becomes free, soaring back to heaven. We are a covenant people, a people dominated by the belief in one transcendent G-d, a G-d who is the Creator and Sustainer of all life with whom we have a special relationship back to Abraham."

Abraham, the old man from an old Chaldean family who left behind the pagan polytheism of his people to establish a new people not through bloodshed or conquests but through a principle—that there is one omnipresent, omniscient invisible power. It was a covenant that wasn't a privilege, the rabbis taught, but of service. Our task was to act as G-d's witnesses to the rest of mankind. It was a culture created by stories because the stories shaped the people. We lived in a system of rules and regulations designed to achieve the total consecration of the community.

I remember how, at first light, I heard my father dabble in

the basin of water, the ritual cleansing where he spilled water on his hands three times in emulation of the high priest as he would do before his service. Then my father put on his arba kanfot, his fringed garment, because it was believed that while one wore the arba kanfot he would be able to ward off unworthy and immoral impulses and abstain from evil. The tzitzit, the fringes, were attached to the four corners of the garment "that you may look upon them and remember all the commandments of the Lord and do them." Properly attired, he opened his Bible and recited the Shema, not loudly, but reverently:

Hear, O Israel, the Lord
our G-d, the Lord is one.

After my father's death, I looked at his cold, shrunken body and saw no sign of him. I hoped his soul had already begun its journey to its new home and its new life. Silently, I said a prayer for the elevation of his soul. I kept my hands busy by sewing fine white linen together, with no hem or knot of any sort, for the shroud. I stitched together the three garments, the shirt, the breeches, and the overgarment with a girdle, white stockings for the legs, a white cap for his head and a cover for his face. I stitched together the garment that would be placed over his shoulders. As I finished the shroud I was unaware of what I was doing or where I was. I simply worked.

A human being, made in the image of G-d, is deserving of respect always, even in death, perhaps especially in death. The rite of washing the body before burial shouldn't commence before the shrouds are ready. Once my father's shrouds were ready, my mother came into the room and cried when she saw me surrounded by my dead father and the white linen. When my aunts and cousins arrived to help prepare the body, there was no conversation except that which was necessary for the preparation. We washed my father's entire body, beginning with his head, with warm water, and his matted, wiry hair was combed to leave his face, peaceful in his deepest sleep, exposed for our love and our tears. As we washed my father he was always half covered by a sheet, as modesty dictated. We took care not to place his body with his face downward because it was a disgraceful position. Instead, we turned him from side to side. He wasted away during his illness, but in death he hung heavy.

Then my father was placed in a standing position, held up by my mother and me, and my aunt poured water from clay pitchers over his head so it ran the length of his body. Egg in its shell was beaten with some wine and used to wash his head. His fingers were closed, his body was dried, and we anointed him with oils and wrapped him in the shrouds with spices. The sweetness of aloe oil and the musky scent of myrrh were heavy in the air. My mother, my aunts, and my cousins sang psalms, their voices heavy and cracking. I couldn't sing because I had no voice. My mother, my cousin, and I lifted my father to the litter that would carry him to his grave, where he would sleep with his fathers, before sundown.

Looking at the remains of my father, wrapped in shrouds, smelling of aloe and myrrh, for the first time in my memory without a prayer on his lips, I understood the bawling women's laments I heard whenever I accompanied other lines of mourners on their way to the grave. I understood the wailing and the thumping of one's fist to the heart. My husband rented his mantle in respect for my father, and it felt as though my flesh tore with the garment.

When I emerged from my mother's room, where the women retreated after becoming ritually unclean from tending to my father's burial preparations, my husband was, in his way, kind and comforting. Through the doorway he spoke to me of his memories of my father, of how he knew my father was a pious man and wouldn't even consider cheating in business.

"He only wanted what was fair," my husband said, as if he still couldn't believe it. "He only wanted what he believed his work earned."

As my father was carried to his tomb at his family gravesite where his ancestors for generations rested, people from all over the village wailed and mourned for him. My father had been much loved. People saw the truth of G-d in him and had clung to him, a simple shepherd, knowing he understood in a way they longed for. These people loved my father, and that's when I first saw G-d in the world, this G-d of love he had told me of again and again.

After my father's funeral I walked through Nazareth. I looked at the open-air shops, saw the sheep grazing in the distance, and breathed in the air of grass and sea. I saw the people who worked hard with calloused-covered hands. They hugged each other, laughed loudly, and cried sincerely. I saw the hearts of the villagers in a way I had never seen when I lived there. My father died and these people, some of them distant acquaintances, rushed to my mother's side to help, such a contrast to the polite formality I found among the wealthy in Jerusalem.

"Woman!" my husband called. "What are you doing walking the streets alone? It isn't respectable. Come back to your mother's house and help her as you should."

I walked toward my husband, and at that moment I realized I was sorry I ever left Nazareth. It was my home, and by denying my home I was denying the truest part of myself. Perhaps that was why I was living in pieces since I'd left. I wished I could go back in time, to when I was a young girl and intent on watching the women in Sepphoris, seeing what they had that I didn't. I wanted to remove myself from the coveting. I wanted to be happy with my life, recognizing my good fortune in my parents and seeing that a good life can be carved from the most difficult of circumstances. But I couldn't turn back the clock no matter how much I wished it. I made my choices. Now I had to live with the consequences.

"It's my home too," I said to my husband. "Nazareth is my home."

My husband laughed. "Yes, you are very much of Nazareth."

I helped my mother serve wine to the men who gathered to take my father's litter to his grave. When the men were served she pulled me aside and whispered. Standing next to her again I felt gratitude to her for teaching me her very wisdom, wisdom of a different sort than my father had. She taught me how to bake bread, and by teaching me to bake bread she showed me how to survive. I remembered when I was a girl and she showed me how to separate a portion of the dough from the rest of the bread, a challah, a heave offering that would be given to the priest, for it is said, "From the first of your dough shall you give unto the Lord as a heave-offering."

"Woman is allowed this holy task of separating the dough because of her origin at the creation of the world," my mother said. "There would be no future generations without her. She was there at the beginning—created from Adam's rib, made from a challah-portion of man. A woman's kitchen is to be a Temple of G-d, her family table an altar. Daughter, remember this always. When you feed someone the bread from your hands you're sharing with them a portion of yourself."

But after my father died she wasn't worrying about the challah portion of bread. "You must be careful," she said. She straightened my red-jeweled necklace so it lay flat around my neck. "I had a vision of you. In a crowd. And it wasn't good. Remember, Daughter, the wages of sin is death."

"I know, Mother. But the sins have already been committed."

"You can choose to no longer sin."

"But my sins are my only reason for living."

As the sun dropped I sat behind my brother's house with my veil close to my face so I wouldn't be recognized. I was starving, dizzy, frightened that every passing shadow was a horror waiting to happen. I had been caught and shamed, the wages of sin is death, they screamed at me. Die sinner die. I wished they had stoned me, finished me. Finally, I left my brother's home and wandered until I stood outside the city gates.

"Unclean! Unclean!" I shouted, reaching my hand out for alms. I was too numb to feel the pain of the public humiliation. Suddenly, I saw the disapproving glare of my sister-in-law and I bowed in shame.

"There's no time for that," she said. "I'm taking you to a friend who is kind and discrete. He and his family will provide for you and give you shelter until you are recovered. Then he will take you back to Nazareth, to the nowhere where you belong."

She walked quickly through the streets and, panting and stumbling, I struggled to keep up with her. Her veil, like mine, was clutched close to her face so she wouldn't be recognized alongside a sinner condemned in the Temple before G-d. She could become unclean simply by my presence, and she didn't touch me. She led me into the suburb of Bezetha where many merchants lived. We stopped before the door of a merchant's house. She knocked on the door and told the servant girl she wanted to see the master. The girl looked at her, at me, and shut the door. My sister-in-law stood in the street as we waited.

"Why are you doing this?" I asked.

"I can't have my husband's sister begging outside the city gates, and that's all you can come to now—a beggar with an outstretched hand. My husband has worked hard to make a success of his business. Do you know what a problem it would be for him if his sister, a sinner known to all the world, is seen begging?"

She left me alone at the door. She went back the way she came, her veil not held so tight now, her shoulders relaxed, her mind at ease. She had done her part. Now she could go home.

ELEVEN

*T*he weather cooled when it neared shearing season. As the days grew shorter, the sheep's wool grew shorter, my father used to say, and the harvest season grew closer. In Nazareth, there was a sense of change, of time passing, unlike in Jerusalem where it wasn't as warm sometimes and the produce and flowers had to be imported from different regions. In Jerusalem, we knew the seasons changed when the crowds rushed into town. During the holidays pilgrims swarmed into the city and prices for food and shelter rose. Jerusalem became so overcrowded that many visitors had to sleep in the hills outside the city gates. The biggest crowds arrived during Passover since the rabbis insisted that Passover could only be righteously celebrated in Jerusalem. Jews from all over the Diaspora, those spread throughout various regions of the Mediterranean, crowded into the walled City of David, the city rebuilt after G-d allowed its destruction, the city with its second temple. This was the place of the Holy of Holies where He Himself presided, and Jews came to worship in hopes of finding Him.

My husband and I, along with his two brothers, traveled 100 miles from my home in Nazareth to his home in Jerusalem where he would accept me as his wife. As we traveled, we went from the shores of the lake to dry ravines and thistles. We passed forests and a blank desert where nothing lived. Under the burning sky the metallic surface of the lake shimmied, and in an hour's travel we passed from the richest plains to the barest hills where sheep grazed. We passed deep valleys, canyon-like gorges, and isolated stretches of high land resembling fortresses. We passed natural caves used for flocks and for men needing to escape.

When I first saw Jerusalem gleaming in the distance I was overtaken with wonder. The rabbis said that he who has never seen Jerusalem has never seen a beautiful city. That is where He lives, my father told me, the One so sacred only the high priest could pronounce His name. I clasped my hands and sighed when I saw the panorama of the gilded Temple glistening. Perhaps this is where I'll find my peace, I thought.

The holy city was at the bottom of a hollow of surrounding hills, a single break in the ring of hills, Wad En-Nar, from where Jerusalem touched the desert. By the time my husband brought me to his home, Jerusalem had been the holy center of G-d's people for ten centuries. King Solomon, son of David, protected his father's city with a wall, the first wall, built upon the western hill. By the time my husband brought me to his home, King Herod the Great, father of the current king, Antipas, had added the final architectural touches as protection by adding a powerful citadel crowned by three enormous towers and he strengthened the Temple with the great Antonia Fortress. When my husband and I stopped to rest on the Mount of Olives, I held my breath. Jerusalem was even larger than I imagined. The city looked like an impregnable fortress, a vast jewel spread over a sea of bronze. Beyond the ravine of

Kidron a wall reared over 250 feet high topped by towers 460 feet tall. Resting upon the foundation of Almighty-sized masonry, the Temple rose in splendor, stretching gilded spires toward G-d Himself, and upon the northern flank stood the immense gleaming cube of the Antonia Fortress. The other ravine was the valley of GeHinnom, the Gehenna of evil memory, where the sight of sacrifices to the pagan god Moloch outraged the holy king Josiah. From that time forward, filth and dead animals were thrown into the pit, and there was a perpetual fire to burn the city's rubbish to remind us of our sinful past.

"This is hell," my husband said, gesturing toward the Dung Gate where flames licked the southern edge of the city. "This is a glimpse of the underworld, sheol, the place of gloom for those unconnected with G-d. The flames are a symbol of the eternal fires. This is what happens to sinners. A lesson for everyone always." The flames licked especially high. "No one dares venture past after nightfall. All sorts of dangers can occur after nightfall."

We entered the city through the Damascus Gate, and I was overwhelmed by the enclosing walls stretching for more than two Roman miles. When I looked over the heights of Jerusalem I saw a gulf of a great rift, at the bottom of which the River Jordan flows toward the Dead Sea. Inside the city, beginning at the Temple, where it merged into the retaining wall of the court, the wall enclosed the mound of Zion, turned above the junction of the GeHinnom and Kidron, climbed the heights as far as the palace-fortress of Herod, made a right turn with the Hippicus Tower at its corner, seemed to go into the town by two redans of which the second bordered Golgotha and then onto the Temple again. The wall was built of enormous blocks, some projecting forward, some pulling back, leaving gaps and projections, strengthened by towers every 100 yards.

As soon as we passed through the gate we were trapped inside a maze of narrow streets that zigzagged between blocks of houses laid out without any plan. Life in Jerusalem was a tightly packed mass where every inch of space was used. The houses clung to one another, overlapping and interpenetrating. There was little green and few gardens except for Herod's garden and the walled garden of roses which, legend said, went back to the time of the prophets. Here and there was a fig tree standing lonely and misplaced in a courtyard. The streets were so narrow that two people walking side by side would have to jostle with other passers-by for space, which caused no end of disputes and arguments. There was no room for carriages, only a few wealthy men's litters, many donkeys with hard hooves tapping on the stones, and it was tiring walking up or down since many of the streets were cut into steps. To my horror, there were long lines of sheep and cattle, sacrificial animals led to the Temple. Always there were scornful Roman troops, wearing their crested helmets and their red shoulder cloaks, mounted soldiers who negotiated the steps with their horses with great difficulty. There were no wide avenues or open spaces, and I thought of the open sky and the pink-red sunsets I was used to in Nazareth. My husband didn't notice my growing concern. I was his wife, we were in public, and we shouldn't be seen communicating. He moved ahead, set on his destination. He knew where he was going, navigating his way through the maze of alleys, lanes, and inner courts.

I followed him through the central hollow of the Tyropoeon, the Valley of Cheesemakers. We crossed the broad causeway and the bridge, which was linked to the Temple and upper town. Below stretched a great paved square bounded on the north by the old palace of the Asmoneans, with its white roofs and colonnades, where Herod Antipas stayed when he resided in Jerusalem for the feasts. We passed the smaller squares, named after certain trades—Square of the Butchers, Wool-Weavers, Fullers, Fishmongers. There was an Upper Market for the upper classes, a Lower Market for the poorer classes. The traders' stalls, lining the streets in the open-air markets, didn't help ease traffic. The strong smells encompassed me and the city reeked with life and death and stages between. Hot cooking grease mingled with the rubbish that was swept from open places every day but left to smolder in the alleys. There were too many noises for my quiet, country brain and my ears hurt making sense of them all. In the fullers' quarter was the dull, monotonous noise of fulling. In the coppersmith's quarter was the rhythmic din of hammering. Tradesmen shouted trying to attract customers, water carriers hollered bearing their skins on their backs and offering their services, the public criers called for silence to make their official announcements, the yelling guards clearing a path for condemned men on their way to Golgotha, carrying the beam of their crosses over their shoulders. I hadn't arrived at my house yet, and I already knew I made a mistake marrying this man and following him to Jerusalem. But it was too late. I was his wife, and this noisy, crowded, unfriendly place was my home.

Years passed from my first arrival in Jerusalem until the autumn morning, so early the sun wasn't yet over the Temple, when my husband was called away. He wasn't bothered when Caiaphas' letter came by messenger. He felt very important being summoned by the high priest, and he would look the part. He dressed quickly into his consecrated clothes, his finest mantle, his tzitzit, his fringed garment, smoothed flat around his shoulders so his shawl would lay perfectly.

"This will be good for me," my husband said as I helped him dress. "I'll be known as someone who the high priest summons when he is in need. I'll be known as someone who helps his people when he is called on."

He walked away, then turned back, as if in afterthought. He was going to say something but turned away, his eyes small, his face toward the Temple. He might have said something to save me, but he walked away.

I watched him leave toward the Temple while I stood on the roof of our home, and I had a presentiment of doom. I thought of the time when I passed GeHennom with him when we made our way to Jerusalem that first time. I thought of the burning pit of flames and terror, the acrid smell of the misused and unheeded. The wind blew from the east and smoke from the altar of the sacrifices stung my nose and scratched my eyes, the horrible reek of burning flesh and the heady smell of incense. It was early morning, still not light enough for sunshine to stream over the Temple, reflecting gilded shimmers over the homes and haphazard streets. I remembered the Jerusalem of my dreams, the Jerusalem I meant to find when I arrived. When I first spotted the city from the distance, I wanted it to be the home of a G-d who loved me and who I would finally understand and love in return. That was my father's dream for me, that I would one day realize that G-d loved me. But the city wasn't what I imagined. My husband wasn't what I imagined. I didn't see the hand of a loving G-d. I only saw mistakes and disappointments.

As the sun rose the city clamored with its cacophony of sounds. The tradesmen were haggling, and the animals being driven to slaughter were bleating. During the afternoon siesta, during the hottest hours of the day, the city quieted only to regain strength and sound that cackled until nightfall. But I couldn't wait until nightfall to see him. I left to find the man I loved to tell him I couldn't be with him any longer. People were seeing, hearing things we meant only for ourselves. I had to tell him I was sure my husband knew, but when I looked into my lover's eyes and touched his smile he was all I wanted.

"I'm not afraid," he said. "There's no way anyone can know of us. Where have they seen us? What have they heard? We've been careful. Even our shadows cannot find us."

"But you said the rabbi has been wanting to have you dismissed from the Temple, disgraced in your profession. What better way to have you released than to prove you're an adulterer?"

I shuddered uncontrollably. He touched my shoulders and tried to still me but I couldn't be stilled. I thought of the girls who were dragged away to be stoned. I thought about the sacrificial animals who screamed at their ends. I thought of my husband and felt the guilt of my betrayal. I thought of my father who would die of shame if he hadn't died already.

"The rabbi and I have come to an understanding," he said. "I'm going to help him in his quest, and he's going to help me in mine."

He's going to help you become a scribe remembered through the ages? I wondered about the glaring eyes the rabbi aimed at him during their dinner conversations and I couldn't understand the rabbi's change of heart.

He read the question in my eyes. "He realizes I can help him so he finds me useful. You and I will be together forever. We'll find a way."

He looked so sincere, and I believed him. Perhaps it was truth in his eyes. Perhaps it was something else. With his arms around me I finally settled, and I began to think of an answer that would suit my husband about where I had been that day.

TWELVE

I may have screamed. I may have cried. I may have grasped for my robes or the blanket. I may have clawed at the skin of the violent hands tearing me away from my dreams. I may have grabbed for him while he may have grabbed for me, but arms stronger and more determined than ours held him pinned and he struggled but couldn't release himself from the many-fisted bandits who forced their way into our sanctuary. The sun was glowing over the city of gold as I was dragged on the floor by men who had dined at my home, men I had served with the bread I baked, men who praised my husband's choice of wife. Now they were fierce, violent, pulling my hair and dragging me through the doorway and out onto the road. They yelled loudly so everyone would hear. Come see the sinner, they said. Come see the woman of stones.

Their faces hardened into indignation as though they wore the tragedy masks of Greek actors. I screamed for my scribe, but he didn't come. I screamed for G-d, for mercy, for the girls dragged through the gates before me and never returned. I screamed for myself because now I was one of them. I saw the hand-sized stones the men gathered as they dragged me toward the Temple. The stones on the ground pounded my arms and legs into bloody contusions. Dirt and sand scratched my eyes while I screamed for my father, who in Heaven must have turned away from his soiled daughter, the one who couldn't control her coveting, the one who never believed. They dragged me, torn and bleeding, down the Temple Court steps. Then my screams were gone and I was left in a heap on the ground, struggling for breath, thinking the sooner I was stoned the better because then my pain would be past and I would be released from the hell of this sinful existence. Two men grabbed my arms and held me upright though my legs crumbled like dust beneath me. Through the haze of my sorrow I saw people sitting around the man who was talking to them. I closed my eyes because I couldn't see them seeing me in my disgrace.

"Teacher," one of my assailants called, his voice boastful, "this woman was caught in the very act of adultery. In the Law, Moses commands us to stone such women. What do you say?"

I sank to my knees. They didn't make me stand again. The teacher sat calmly, unperturbed by the insistent questions my accusers threw at him as they would soon hurl stones at me.

Finally, the teacher looked at me. "If any one of you is without sin let him cast the first stone."

I pulled myself into a ball, eyes closed tight. If I couldn't see the stones hurling with death-force toward me then perhaps they wouldn't hurt when they collided with my flesh and bones. But I heard no accusations. I felt no stones. When I opened my eyes my accusers were gone.

"Woman," he asked, "where are they? Has no one condemned you?"

"No, sir," I said.

"Nor do I. Now go your way and sin no more."

I DREW my mat toward the warmth of the sunshine, pulling it from side to side, watching the goldenrod rays as they filtered through the window high in the wall. I was cold, so cold, and by pulling my mat around and around I thought I could find the warmth my body longed for.

"It's not cold," the wife of my caretaker said when I asked for another quilt, and then another. "It's only harvest time. It's cooler," she said, "but not cold."

But I was so cold. I thought it was the rush flooding me then, wondering where he was, my lover, what he was doing, where he had gone. He wasn't dragged before the teacher though he, too, committed a death-sin by bedding a married woman. Without pain or longing I wondered if he had done something to allow his dream of becoming a scribe for the ages to come true. I wondered if he sacrificed me, or if he was also a victim. I would never know because I never saw him again. As time passed I would think about him without malice. Since I didn't know the truth about his actions I could invent a story that suited me, and I chose to believe he loved me.

Nima found me at my caretaker's. She knew I could never go back to my husband's house. He made a show of denouncing me, his harlot wife, by dumping my belongings into the street outside the home we had shared, publicly proclaiming me to be the sinner I was, as someone who should have been stoned, would have been stoned if that man hadn't been in the way. My husband was enraged, and rightfully so. He said my name would be erased from the Book of Life and I wouldn't sleep with my ancestors. When no one was looking, Nima gathered as many of my belongings as she could carry and brought them to me. I didn't want anything from that life, from those choices, but I thanked Nima because she risked herself to try to salvage some of myself for me. But there was nothing left to salvage. I hadn't been stoned yet I was torn to bits inside. I hadn't died but I was lost forever to the pious.

I stayed on my mat, still watching the sunlight trickle through the window, pointing finger rays of derision at me, illuminating my sins from the heavenly skies, leaving me wondering at the madness of it all. The husband I married wasn't the husband of my heart. The man I loved was unreachable to me and should have stayed unreachable except in my weakness I thought it would be all right because love must make it right. If what I felt for my husband was distant affection and what I felt for my lover was emotional connection combined with lust, then where was this love I had searched for all my life? Where was this love I dreamed of? I knew the law, had the verses from Deuteronomy memorized, because I thought knowing the consequences would deter me from doing what I knew was wrong. I never meant to do wrong, but his arms were so warm.

Then I thought of the teacher. Sitting alone, outside the circle of priests and rabbis pointing their fingers and yelling about my disgrace. A woman who sinned was worse than a man who sinned because a man was just a man but a woman was the mother of future generations. The teacher offered forgiveness, and if I accepted the forgiveness then it was mine.

"Sin no more," he said. "Sin no more."

I had my life back. I wanted to accept this gift of rebirth as fully as possible. In a moment, quick as a flash, I saw my father's face and I understood what he had been trying to teach me all along. I had a hole in my heart that I had tried to fill every other way, by keeping busy, baking bread, and being loved by a man who was not my husband. Suddenly, I saw the

G-d of love my father always knew. I saw his smile in the pattern of the sunlight.

Of all the religious duties women were excused from, we weren't excused from the most important of all—repentance. With a contrite spirit and a broken heart, I repented of my sins, which were many: coveting a life that wasn't mine, coveting a man who wouldn't make me happy, coveting a man who could make me happy when I was married to another, coveting secrets and lies and a life that wasn't meant to be. I prayed and prayed, back and forth, back and forth, G-d, my G-d, the G-d of love my father was now personally acquainted with, back and forth, back and forth, I swayed myself into a mesmerized pattern of tear-streaked repentance, back and forth. I had to be forgiven. I needed G-d to forgive me for my vanity, my selfishness, my greed, my dishonesty, my covetousness. I prayed aloud until I had no voice left. I prayed until there was nothing left to say. And then, as though the weight of the world had been lifted from my shoulders, I felt lighter somehow but I needed to be forgiven.

I had to find him. He had given me my life back. He might help me find the forgiveness I desperately needed. Although adultery is the greatest sin a woman can commit, I thought I would hurt no one with my transgressions. I thought I could have what I wanted, and the man I loved could have what he wanted, and my husband would never know. No one would ever know—foolish reasoning since people in Jerusalem knew everything about everyone. I asked Nima to inquire about the rabbi from Nazareth. She discovered that he had gone to break bread with a noted rabbi, a man with whom my husband had dined many times.

I wore Nima's clothing, pulling her veil over my face. I grabbed my finest alabaster jar of expensive nard from India, a last relic of my former life reclaimed by Nima, and I opened the door and walked into the street. It was the first time I had left the safety of the house since the incident and the fine autumn sunlight burned my eyes. I walked to the Pharisee's house and when I arrived I didn't knock. I didn't think. I let myself in and saw the men reclining around the table.

I didn't intend to weep but all I could think about was the violence he saved me from. I washed his feet with the tears of my gratitude and then I bowed low before him, my forehead to the floor, my tumbling hair drying his feet. I perfumed his feet with nard, the odor penetrating the house with musk and sorrow. I had been dragged from a bed that wasn't mine, yet even at my worst, beneath the smeared tears and bloody bruises, my inherent worth was there for all to see. Suddenly, with everyone in the room staring at me, I understood my value and it wasn't attached to any man. The value was all my own. The realization was blinding in its clarity.

The Pharisee wasn't pleased. His stone face betrayed his thoughts though his mouth stayed silent. If this man is so wise then he wouldn't allow me to touch him, I sensed the Pharisee thinking. I was a sinner, the Woman of Stones, and my touch made the teacher unclean. The Pharisee was ready to send me away in further disgrace.

"Simon," the rabbi from Nazareth said, "I have something to tell you."

"Tell me," the Pharisee said.

"Two men owed money to a certain moneylender. One owed him five hundred denarii and the other fifty. Neither of them had the money to pay him back so he cancelled the debts of both. Now which of them will love him more?"

The Pharisee said, "The one who owed him more debt."

"Yes." He turned to me. "Do you see this woman? I came into your house. You didn't give me any water for my feet but she bathes them with her tears and dries them with her hair.

You didn't put oil on my head but she has perfumed my feet. Her sins have been forgiven because she loves much. But who has been forgiven little loves little." He nodded at me. "Your sins have been forgiven. Go in peace."

I wandered outside and saw the arched Damascus Gate that led toward Damascus and Galilee, the one that led toward Nazareth—home. I thought of the Golden Gate, the most impressive gate in the east, the one that led directly to the Temple, the one through which many believed Messiah would come from the summit of the Mount of Olives, the pillars of which were believed to have been a gift from the Queen of Sheba to Solomon. I knew where the Fountain Gate opened to the south and led toward the Kidron. I knew where the Zion Gate stood, on Mount Zion near the tomb of King David. I knew where the Sheep Gate was near the sheep market, where the sacrificial sheep were led toward the Temple because men couldn't or wouldn't learn without shedding blood. I wouldn't go there, and I wouldn't go near the Dung Gate. I had already been in the eternal fires, seen it, lived it, escaped it. I didn't yet know which gate to use but all were available to me. Whichever gate I did choose I knew I would be a different woman from then on. I reached toward my throat and realized the necklace of blood-red stones no longer hung like a chain around my neck. It must have been lost in the chaos of my struggle.

I heard my father's voice say, "You are free."

I walked away from my accusers, my husband, my lover, away from Jerusalem forever with my head held high. "Abba, I understand."

Then I heard my father's favorite line from his favorite psalm, in his voice:

"Be still and know that I am G-d."

And I did.

I spent my life wanting to be loved, failing to see I always was. I was loved with the divine love that understands, forgives, and gives the strength to carry on even through adversity and pain.

IF I BEGIN at the beginning, as all parables begin at the beginning, you will see why I was born to be what I am. You can see how I was molded from clay into permanent infamy. You can see why I was born to be a lesson for everyone always, why I was born to do wrong so you would do right. Why I was born to be judged so you would not judge. You have seen the places where stones have marked my life, stones as memories handed down, handed over, passed around, stones used to cover the graves where our loved ones wait for us in eternity, the stones we leave by their graves to show we are here, we remember. I lived my life grasping at stones, whether rough like the stones in the ravines of Nazareth or smooth like the sky-blue stone my lover gave me in Jerusalem, a solid remembrance of him. I had seen stones as harsh, gritty, jagged. I had forgotten that the lapis lazuli was also a stone, rubies and diamonds are also stones, precious jewels that bring iridescent beauty to the world. I had forgotten that even the most jagged cuts become smooth when sanded.

Every life is a parable, a story lived in metaphors and allegories to show others the path toward their best lives. Every life has choices that are complex and thorny. Sometimes there isn't one right answer, only two wrong ones. Still, every life has lessons to teach, and if we're willing to learn we'll find ourselves more whole. We may even begin to understand what we most need to learn. And when we hear that G-d is love, G-d is love, we must listen and learn.

There is no other way.

ABOUT THE AUTHOR

Meredith Allard is an award-winning author known for the bestselling *Loving Husband Trilogy* and the Victorian novel *When It Rained at Hembry Castle*, which IndieReader named a Best Historical Novel. Her prequel, *Down Salem Way*, earned the B.R.A.G. Medallion and was a semi-finalist for the Chaucer Award in Early Historical Fiction.

A recognized authority on the craft, Meredith is the author of *Painting the Past: A Guide for Writing Historical Fiction*, a #1 Amazon New Release in Authorship and Creativity Self-Help. For over twenty years, she has mentored writers of all ages, helping them find their voices while honing her own signature blend of meticulous research and haunting prose.

When she isn't unearthing the secrets of the past, she can be found in the hills of Southern Nevada with her cats and a cup of coffee.

Join Meredith online at www.meredithallard.com for her weekly blog posts and monthly newsletter.

BOOKS BY MEREDITH ALLARD

And Shadows Will Fall

Christmas at Hembry Castle

Down Salem Way

The Duchess of Idaho

Her Dear & Loving Husband

Her Loving Husband's Curse

Her Loving Husband's Return

Painting the Past: A Guide for Writing Historical Fiction

The Professor of Eventide

The Swirl and Swing of Words: Embracing the Writing Life

Victory Garden

When It Rained at Hembry Castle

Woman of Stones